TELL THEM THAT I'M COMING

INTERNATIONAL BESTSELLING AUTHOR

SARAH SPADE

Copyright © 2026 by Sarah Spade

All rights reserved.

No part of this book may be reproduced in any form or by any electronic or mechanical means, including information storage and retrieval systems, without written permission from the author, except for the use of brief quotations in a book review.

Cover by Fran of Merry Book Round

Art by _Azuru, S.J. Gautreaux of Night Witchery, Ariel Illustration

FOREWORD

Thank you for checking out *Tell Them That I'm Coming,* the next entry in the **Sombra Demons** universe!

From the moment that Shannon discovered she was pregnant in *Santa Claws,* I was wondering what a half demon, half human child would be like — and what kind of story they could have. Of course, when it comes to Alana, she already was featured in a prophecy that led to her saving her father's demon realm before she was even a year old. And *that* led me to wonder: what would happen if you grew up, knowing you did what you were born to do before you could even remember it… and what if there's a *second* prophecy about you that you just don't know yet?

That was the inspiration for her story. This is more of a romantasy than a monster romance since Alana's hero is a fae bandit who is my take on a charming, Robin Hood-esque character, and it brings us to the hidden world of Noctavara that was briefly mentioned at the end of the final book of the main **Sombra Demons** series, *Shannon in Sombra*. Set twenty-five years after that book, Alana is all grown up, and she's getting her own romance!

This is a single POV book — another difference between this spin-off and the original series — with all of the humor, heart, and adventure from the main series, plus a possessive hero that's head-over-heels for the heroine (even when he's spent his entire existence believing that his type of fae is cursed to never find true love…). As a romantasy, the story is definitely a slow burn with a single open door scene, but because it's written in the same vein as a **Sombra Demons** story, it's fast-paced and a quick (and hopefully) fun read!

I hope you enjoy!

xoxo,
Sarah

PROPHECY

Her path is to save Sombra, but never stay,
her fate tied to the one with
a shadow for a heart, a gilded touch,
and the wrong way…
For her broken wings will only end the curse
when her own heart stops.

CHAPTER 1
BUTTERFLIES

Whenever anyone in Nuit is looking for me, they just have to follow the butterflies.

They glow softly as they drift through the air, white wings catching the light of the dark moon, settling on the log or stone or whatever I'm on or even just perching atop my knee like they belong there. Like they belong wherever I am. Others might circle lazily near my head, unbothered by the way some of the villagers pause in awe when they see them—when they see *me*.

No wonder I tend to spend most of my time in Nuit on the edge of it. After twenty-five years, you'd think I'd get used to the stares, to the murmurs, to my clansmen nodding in gratitude for something that I'll never be able to remember…

Sitting on his haunches, Binx flicks his tail once at my ankle before curling it around his forelegs.

"I know," I murmur, without looking down. "It's annoying."

The butterflies don't listen. They never do. They just keep gathering, soft and persistent, until anyone with half a brain in Nuit knows exactly where I am.

Of course my soul-pet is with me, too. The butterflies always seem to appear, especially when I'm in one of my moods, but Binx… my childhood as Nuit's savior isn't the only thing I don't remember. I couldn't tell you how Binx chose me to bond with. Ever since I was a wee spawn, the ungez has been there, my guardian and my friend. We have a bond that will only rival the one I eventually share with my mate, but while ungez can't speak—not Sombran, not Human—I usually understand him anyway.

It's an ungez thing. Just like his triangle-shaped ears, glowing white eyes, sharp claws, shadow fur, and fluffy tail, Binx—named by Mom, who told me he reminded her of a cross between two Earth creatures, a cat and a squirrel, and picked a name that reminded her of a black cat from her childhood because of it—are parts of what makes him an ungez, so is his innate ability to choose one soul to bond with. He picked spawn Alana when she was barely big enough to crawl. It's a gift, and I love him. I also love how no one else knows what the flick of his ear, the swish of his tail, or the chittering sound coming from behind his sharp teeth means except for me.

Most of all, I love how he loves me because I'm me, not because of any old prophecies and unfulfilled expectations now that I'm grown…

Right now, he's wondering why I've slunk out into the ash fields, watching the black and white and grey ash glow with vibrant red heat, the fires burning in the distance before being swallowed up by Sombra's shadows. To the right, there's the path that leads to the lava pools, but I have my back to it so that hopefully none of the other villagers notice me hiding away from the rest of the clan.

Especially since I'm not really supposed to be here in Nuit at the moment.

See, I told Mom that I was visiting the neighboring plane of Brille Rouge with Rafe earlier this morning. She doesn't like it, but as I'm twenty-five years old now, she admits that I *am* mature enough to use my powers if I choose to. Of the four halflings— half-human, half-demon—who live in our village, I'm the only one who has the gift of walking through shadows and traveling to nearby realms. I've traveled to countless ones, even those that no one in Sombra has heard of before I stepped foot on their land, but after I recently discovered I was blocked from one world in particular, I've found I've lost a taste for it.

That was two gold moons ago. Since then, I've used my shadows to bring Rafe to Brille Rouge whenever Mom doesn't need me at the EL or Rafe has an afternoon off from lessons with his mage father, Loki.

Like this morning.

I don't mind working with Mom at the Earth Library. Her friend, Amy, usually brings new books written in Human—Mom's language—whenever she visits Nuit with her mate, Nox, so there's always something new to read and to offer to the demons and demonesses that have learned Human. I'm lucky. Part human myself, I was taught it from the cradle, same as Sombran. Mom and Loki's mother, Kennedy, have spent my whole life teaching it to anyone in the clan who was interested, and now more of Nuit knows Human than doesn't.

Of course, that's because most of the villagers have a fondness for the human women who came to Sombra with their mates before I was born… and because it was a half-human spawn that saved their realm a few gold moons after that.

I sigh.

I could be in Brille Rouge. I brought Rafe there hours ago so that he can continue wooing the pretty seamstress he aims to make his mate, but there's a Human saying Mom's fond of: two's company, three's a crowd. I left Rafe with Katrin before promising I'd return with a portal to bring him home, then high-tailed it back to Sombra myself.

Now I'm sitting on the low stone wall at the edge of the village, boots dangling over the ash, a hint of my shadows curled around the toes. Nuit is quiet this time of day; safe, as it always is. *Protected.* That word follows me nearly as faithfully as the butterflies do.

I saved Sombra, and in return, it seems as if the whole realm wants to make sure that I'm just as protected. Mom, especially, and Dad, too, but when even the most ancient of my clansmen goes out of their way to thank me for something I did when I was an infant, it's no surprise that I find excuses to hide away from the rest of the village.

But the butterflies follow me, and that's all you have to know if you want to track me down—

A soft, lyrical voice interrupts my thoughts.

"Brooding again, are we, Alana?"

I glance sideways as Stevie tucks the skirts of her dress beneath her, then drops down beside me, close enough that her delicate shoulder bumps mine. She doesn't look at the butterflies. She never does once she's near, and I love her for it.

"I'm not brooding," I say. "I'm thinking."

Stevie hums, careful not to use her brand of magic in the sound. Ever since we were spawn, she promised not to enchant Rafe and me with her voice, and now that she's mature, she rarely uses her gift.

Unlike me.

"You look like you're plotting your escape," she points out.

If only I could. Despite having the ability to visit nearly every other realm, I feel trapped in Sombra. I don't tell her that, though. I don't have to. A halfling like me, forever struggling to fit in, she knows exactly how I feel.

So, instead, I give her a crooked grin. "That's just my face."

She snorts and leans back on her hands, gaze sweeping the empty ash fields. "You could move, you know. Make them work a little harder to follow you."

I glance at the butterflies swarming nearby, then shrug. "Why? They'd just find me again."

Stevie makes a soft sound in the back of her throat, an almost agreement that also tells me that she wasn't specifically talking about the butterflies.

Up until three gold moons ago, she was as determined to see beyond Nuit as I was. And then, when one of Duke Haures's soldiers came to Nuit to speak to Glaine—the head of the duke's guard who, along with his human mate, Billie, spends half their time in Nuit and the other in the duke's capital city of Mavro —and saw Stevie walking through the village square.

All of us halflings have different physical features that we got from our parents. Take me, for example. I have Mom's colorless skin, Dad's golden eyes, Mom's pale yellow hair that's closer to white, and Dad's black horns even if mine are barely an inch long. Stevie favors her dad over her mother. Dagon is a fierce hunter with the standard deep red Sombran skin and vivid red eyes. Stevie's flesh is more of a rosy pink with his black hair and red eyes; as a nod to her human mother, she plaits her thick black hair and lets it settle over her shoulders. Her horns are delicate and sharp, her body curvy, and her voice magical… but she didn't even need to utter a single note before Corbin was kneeling before her, telling her that she was his one true mate.

Most Sombra demons have to wait centuries before they chance upon their one true mate. No one knew what to expect for us halflings. After all, I'm the first one that's part human, part demon that's ever been born. I kind of understand Rafe's desire to choose his own mate to soothe his loneliness, but I've always known I'd hold out for my fated mate if I ever took one.

And then Stevie found hers already, barely a quarter of a century into her existence. Mom thinks it's because humans usually find their mates early. She was only a few years older than I am now when she bonded with Dad, so though our parents all think of us as spawn still, it wasn't such a shock that Corbin recognized Stevie as his—or that she agreed that she felt the same pull toward him.

They haven't bonded yet. Three gold moons have passed, with Corbin doing his best to woo Stevie in between his duty to Duke Haures, and I know exactly why Stevie is holding off on agreeing to be his for eternity.

It's that word right there. *Eternity*. She's not even fully twenty-five yet, while Corbin is two hundred and twelve, and she wants to get to know him before she promises him forever. And, sure, all she has to do is give him her essence—the part of a demon that's everything they are, including thoughts, memories, hopes, and dreams—and take his for a mated pair to know everything about one another. She could do that, but while Stevie favors her father's looks, her personality is much closer to Sierra, her human mother.

Stevie wants Corbin to prove himself to her, and I don't blame her. If I ever found my fated mate, I hoped I'd be able to ignore my libido long enough to make sure he's the male for me rather than just fool- ishly trusting that the gods got it right.

Even so, both Rafe and I have spent the last few months asking Stevie what it was like to look in Corbin's green eyes and *know* that he was the male meant for her. She's explained it the best she can, calling it a 'gut punch', and telling us when it happens to us, *we*'ll know.

Rafe doesn't want to wait. He wants it to happen now, and if it doesn't? He'll be happy if the demoness he has his eye on will accept him as her mate before Stevie finally bonds with Corbin.

And then there's me. At the rate I'm going, Clara will be happily bonded before I am, and she's still a spawn. And with Kennedy growing another one of her own in her belly, I might still be sitting out back with Binx when the latest villager in Nuit matures and goes searching for *their* mate…

Sensing my frustrations, Binx climbs to his paws. He scampers up my skirts, curling in my lap.

Stevie leans over, running her fingers through his fur. She doesn't have an ungez—she's never wanted one—but she grew up around Binx. He tolerates her pets in a way he doesn't Rafe's, and he purrs softly beneath Stevie's claws.

"Corbin offered to find me an ungez of my own," she murmurs. "I told him I'd rather one of the fabled blue flowers in the duchess's private gardens. My dad told me how beautiful it was when he served as Duchess Susanna's personal guard. If Corbin can figure out how to bring me one, I told him I'll bond with him before the next gold moon."

Corbin is a full-blooded Sombran soldier who's been lost for Stevie since the moment he genuflected in front of her. I have no doubt in my mind that, to get Stevie to choose him, he'll find a way into the oasis near Duke Haures's palace. Especially since Duchess Susanna is also a human—the first to come to Sombra ages ago—and is a romantic at heart. If Corbin tells the duchess it's for his mate, she'll probably pluck the flower herself.

I've only met the duchess a few times. Like every other Sombra demon male, Duke Haures is too over-protective to allow her to leave Mavro. I know enough about her, though, since she is kin to Mom's close human friend, Amy. Plus, due to my status as the chosen spawn who fulfilled a prophecy and saved Sombra, I've spent more than enough time with the duke.

He believes I'm to thank for breaking the mad king's hold on the shadows, saving his people, and eventually leading him and his mate to bring three royal halflings into existence. Why? Because my birth —that of the first ever human-demon halfling— brought the rain that threatened to snuff out Sombra's fires, but somehow I managed to defeat him and save the entire demon realm, finishing off a prophecy that had been foretold nearly two thousand years before.

I don't know the whole story. Mom's kept most of it hidden, only admitting that I was abducted as a baby and captured by King Yelios, and that when she got me back, the rains stopped and Sombra was saved. As I grew older, I also grew resentful of anything to do with my past and a prophecy I'll never quite understand.

You see, my whole life, I've known that I was the child of prophecy. Half-human, half-demon, I was only four months old when I supposedly saved the world. Twenty-five years later, I strive to have a future when I've already done what I was born to do.

I'm not bitter. I'm not. Just because Stevie is one flower away from forever, and Rafe is almost there, and I feel like I'm stuck in a rut, not belonging to any of the worlds I've spent so long visiting…

I shake my head, sending a few of the butterflies fluttering away. "That's great, Stevie. Congratulations."

She shrugs. "He's a good male. I probably would've already accepted his claim if Mom didn't bring me to Earth for the first gold moon so that I could decide for myself instead of letting my cunt do the thinking for me."

I snort. "Your mom's smart."

"Sometimes," Stevie allows. "She said that just because her generation had to accept their mates before the first gold moon, that doesn't mean I had to."

True. That's the duke's first law. Humans aren't supposed to know about demons unless they're a mate, and even then they must finalize their bond before the gold moon shines. My parents almost missed the deadline because, well, *Mom*, but if a pair of mates are in Sombra instead of hiding out on Earth, they can take as long as they'd like to bond.

Not like it's easy. The gods give us our one true mates because they *want* us to bond our essences together. I'm surprised Stevie's held out this long, but like I said, that's the human in her.

Just like Rafe's insistence that he'd rather have any mate than resign himself to searching for centuries might be the human in *him*.

"Where's Corbin?" I ask. "Is he back at the barracks then?"

"For a couple of days. I figure he'll visit me with the flower as soon as he can." She jerks her chin at me. "What about Rafe? When I saw the butterflies heading this way, I thought I'd find you both here."

"Nah. He's probably reciting poetry to Katrin about now."

Stevie chuckles under her breath. "Poor Katrin."

"It's okay. He likes to put Human words into it to impress her. She has no idea what he's saying half the time."

"That's Rafe for you. Just like how he completely forgot about his lessons with Loki today."

I swivel my head, the quick motion spooking Binx. He chitters in rebuke, settling down again as I run my claws over his fluffy tail. "What do you mean?"

"I ran into Kennedy when I was passing the EL." The Earth Library. "She heard from your mom that the two of you were visiting Brille Rouge today, but that couldn't be right since he was supposed to meet his father this morning."

Shit. It's a Human curse world, one of Mom's favorites, and pretty damn apt at the moment. "He told me he had the whole day to spend with Katrin."

All the more reason why I ducked out and returned home earlier. I told him I'd come back for him between our midday meal and supper. With Kennedy *knocked up* again—another Human phrase, meaning she's with spawn—she insists that Rafe sit down and have supper with Kennedy, Loki, and Kennedy's ungez, Freya, every eve.

There are hours to go, but if I know Kennedy, she's already searching for Rafe. And once she figures out that I used my shadows to bring him to his pretty demoness, she'll be searching for *me*.

In my opinion, Rafe's mother worries too much. She's also convinced that if Rafe is missing—or distracted, or late, or simply breathing wrong—it somehow involves me.

And, for the most part, she's right. While mages can open portals to other realms with Duke Haures's permission, I'm the only one who can take my shadows anywhere, and no one even tries to stop me.

Another way that Alana of Sombra is *different*, though, if I get on the wrong side of Kennedy, I might find someone who finally won't treat me with undeserved reverence every time they see me.

And then Stevie says, "She was leaving the EL when I first saw the butterflies on the edge of the village. If I could follow them, so could she."

I nudge Binx's rump. "Up, Binx."

Stevie raises her eyebrows at me. Unlike full demons, we don't have the ridges over our brows, and the furry strips over our eyes are something we got from our human heritage. "Where are you going?"

"Wherever Rafe's mother isn't," I tell her.

I like Kennedy. Honest. She's so close to my

mother, it's like she's my kin. They run the Earth Library together, had their first—and in Mom's case, *only*—spawn at the same time, giving me my best friend, but if it comes down to snitching on Rafe to his mother or buying him a little more time to woo Katrin before I grab him by his pointed ear and drag him back to Nuit, I know who has my loyalty.

"Running away, Alana?"

"Consider it a strategic withdrawal."

A soldier's mate, Stevie laughs as I give her a wave, heading toward the path that leads to the lava pools, Binx at my feet. "You can't avoid her forever, Alana."

I can't, but that doesn't mean I'm not going to give it a good try.

Heading to the lava pools was smart. There's an unspoken rule in Nuit that, whenever one of the clan is bathing in the warm springs made up of the lava beneath the ash fields, they deserve their privacy. Mainly because mated pairs enjoy the pools together, and if I know for a fact that my parents frequent the pools themselves, I try not to think about that.

At home, we have a bathtub that's large enough to fit my father. He's more than a head-and-a-half taller than me—not counting his horns—and nearly twice as wide, which means that when I have a soak, I can stretch out. Mom? She can basically *swim* in there.

Being close with the village mage is a perk. Loki cast a spell to make the enchanted water as warm as the lava pools, but there's nothing like dipping a toe into the lava itself. It speaks to the demoness in me.

And, no, I wasn't stalling at all. Promise.

I kept waiting for Kennedy to appear at the edge of the ash field that leads to the pools. Loki's human mother is smaller than mine, with hair that's darker, and a bump that tells all of Nuit she is expecting again. If just to ask me if I know what's become of her son, I wait for her to appear. She doesn't. Whether that's because she respects the privacy owed to a bather or because even the butterflies do, it's just Binx and me for a while. The butterflies all dispersed once I started to remove my boots, my dress, and my undercoverings. They'll manifest again—they always do—but for the moment, at least, there's peace.

I don't know why they chase me. To be honest, most of the clan has always seemed more in awe of the butterflies than me. I once asked Mom, but she didn't know. It was actually Lilith, the clanmother and Apollyon's bonded mate, who explained that such a shadow creature used to belong to Queen Alana, the fearsome demoness queen that my father named me after.

She perished more than two millennia ago, right before Duke Haures took the crystal crown that marks him as Sombra's ruler. There hasn't been a single butterfly—or faripoz, as they're known in Sombran— in the centuries since… until one appeared after I was abducted, leading Mom and the others to find me.

One became two became three until, over the years, there have been too many to count. There's usually at least a pair whenever I'm in Sombra. I haven't seen any in the other realms—demon or not—that I've visited with Rafe. Sometimes I wonder why, but when all they do is flap their wings and help keep me calm, it doesn't matter if they're there or not.

Unless someone gapes at them—and me.

Unless they give away where I might be hiding at any given moment.

Unless they're just another reminder that I'm a sorry replacement for the original Queen Alana…

Ugh. I think Stevie was right. I am brooding. It's my fault, too. I get like this when my shadows start thickening, urging me to go on another journey. It's my power. I'm made to travel, and except for popping into Brille Rouge, I haven't gone anywhere in ages. Not even Earth, though Mom's suggested we visit some place called Lon-done. It's like I'm trapped, and if that's me also brooding over how I tried to visit a fire demon realm only to be blocked from it, that's better than the loneliness I can't deny.

I shouldn't be lonely. I have Binx, right? Stevie, too, when she isn't with Corbin. Rafe is usually my shadow, and when Billie and Glaine come to Nuit with Clara, she joins our trio so that we can make sure our youngest halfling is pampered. When Kennedy births her latest spawn, I'm sure we'll treat the newest halfling in Nuit the same, and then if Stevie mates with Corbin…

Binx is curled up along the edge of my lava pool,

paws digging into the ash as I start to climb out of it. I shake off the excess lava, taking my long hair down from the twist I'd put it up in before I waded into the pool.

If I were a full-blooded human, I wouldn't survive the lava pools. Mom has to disappear in Dad's shadows to enjoy the sensation of the heat and the thickness swirling around her skin. Being a half-demon means that the fire doesn't touch me. It's closer to the enchanted water that comes from the tap, soothing my skin and helping me relax.

I don't have the same sort of shadows as my father. Dad has two forms: his solid, red-skinned shape, and his nearly transparent shadows where he's all black except for his golden eyes. When we're on Earth, taking a family trip to Mom's world, we can vanish to mist, all but invisible to the mortal eye. Here? He's either inky black or red and strapping.

Not me. I'm solid, like Mom, with flesh as pale as hers. My shadows hover near my feet, always prepared to be summoned. When I want to tap into my gift, I build a portal out of those shadows and walk right through them. That doesn't mean I can create portals to skip around Sombra. Nope. I can only break through barriers between realms, going from one world to another.

Would be nice if I had the same abilities as the mages do. Rafe's dad can open a portal in Nuit and take a traveler straight into the duke's throne room, all thanks to his brand of magic. Me? I have to settle for dressing again, giving Binx a scratch behind his ears, and walking back to the village square.

I still live with my parents. Of course I do. It's how it's done in Sombra. Until I leave my village or find a mate, my parents are responsible for me. If I wanted to build a den of my own, it would have to be far from my birth clan, where I would be declaring myself a single demoness in search of a mate.

I'm not looking for a male. Not really. I just want to have a purpose, to be more than the child of prophecy who saved Sombra, only for me to find myself looking at an eternity of the same days over and over again.

Maybe I should take a walk into Soleil. Or…. or that djinn realm that had Dad frowning when I mentioned I'd visited that world. Something. *Anything.* I could kill a little time—because gods know I have an endless amount of it—and then retrieve Rafe from Brille Rouge before supper.

That seems like a good plan. I'll take Binx for company, and if I'm gone, Kennedy won't be able to blame me for abandoning her precious spawn in the arms of the seamstress seductress who is allowing Rafe to woo her.

Is Katrin Rafe's mate? Not his one true mate for sure, but if he sees forever with her, who am I to interfere? Kennedy will understand. That's what Mom says. She admits that Kennedy is a little too overprotective when it comes to Rafe, and considering Shannon is *my* mom, that's saying something.

Now, I love my mom. She's got a good heart, a smart mouth, and she does a great job running the Earth Library with Kennedy. She makes my dad happy, she's devoted to us both, but, gods, she treats me like I'm still a child.

If Kennedy is trying to hunt down Rafe, Mom must be at the EL. As the clan's artist, Dad's been working on a new mural in Kennedy and Loki's home, preparing for the new spawn. He's spent the last couple of moons working on it during the days so that he's home every eve with Mom and me.

That's why, as I approach our home from the back, I'm stunned to hear his gravely voice trying to soothe Mom's more frantic, high-pitched tone. The window on the side is open, their voices carrying, and I know instinctively that they're in the front room, Mom pacing, Dad hovering nearby to lend her his quiet strength as she tells him whatever is bothering her.

Me. It's always me.

"—Brille Rouge again."

"Yes, my Shannon," murmurs Dad. "Alana told you that she was visiting the demonesses with Rafe. Remember? Over breakfast."

Mom continues as though Dad didn't speak up at all. "I told Ken that it's hormones. Rafe knows better than to throw away his essence for a demoness who isn't his one true mate. She's so worried about him choosing the wrong mate. And, of course, it's our baby who's bringing him there instead of staying in Sombra where she belongs."

Belonging in both worlds, belonging in none…

"Alana is a good friend. Besides, it's only Brille Rouge. It's not Noctavara."

Noctavara.

A shiver runs down my spine, my heart tripping over itself to hear the name of the one realm that refused to let me enter. Why are they talking about Noctavara now?

I inch closer, ducking my head so that they can't see me. Normally, Dad can sense when I'm near because I'm made up of his essence and Mom's—not to mention his demon sense of hearing and smell that poor Mom doesn't have despite being bonded to him —but when Mom's in one of these moods, she has all of his attention.

He adores her. When I think of my Dad, I want a mate who loves me unconditionally like my parents love each other. Especially since, when I'm cavesdropping, it's a whole lot easier when he's distracted by Mom…

"I know. And I'm being ridiculous, Mal. If it's blocked to her, it's not like Alana can go there even if she wants to. But the doppelseers…"

"Lucian and Damien saw what our daughter would do thousands of years before she was born to do it. We could have centuries before the second prophecy comes to pass.”

I blink. At my feet, Binx lets out a soft mewing sound, checking to make sure that I’m all right.

But I’m not all right.

Second prophecy? What?

Mom shudders out a breath. “Sierra’s girl found her mate. Oh, Malphas, don’t look at me like that. Everyone in Nuit knows it’s only a matter of time before Corbin has Stevie’s name etched in his chest. And we all know that Kennedy’s son is trying. How much longer until Alana goes searching and Damien’s words catch up to her?”

“Fiore mi…”

“You heard what he said. If she goes to Noctavara…” Mom pauses, and when she speaks again, it’s obvious she’s reciting something. “‘Her broken wings will only end the curse when her own heart stops’.”

“My flower, you remember the prophecy so easily?”

“Of course I do! When a seer looks at your baby and tells you that there’s a second prophecy about her, as a mother, you remember that shit, babe. Especially when it talks about her heart stopping to break someone else’s curse.”

“It could mean something else,” Dad says calmly. Like always.

“Does it matter? They see Alana leaving Sombra.

They see her *dying*." Mom's voice breaks. And, yes, that's not unusual, either. "We can't let her go to Noctavara."

I lift up just enough to peek through the window in time to see Dad enveloping Mom in a big hug. Her pale yellow hair stands out against his deep red chest as he strokes the strands.

"Alana is your daughter, my Shannon. Do you think we could ever stop her?"

IF I NEVER HEAR THE WORD 'PROPHECY' AGAIN, IT'LL be too soon.

I can't. I just… I *can't*.

Mere moments ago, I was bemoaning how stagnant my immortal life felt. I figured that was something that happens to young demons as they mature. The idea of a never-ending forever is daunting, especially for a halfling. My mom is in her seventh decade. Dad's seen more than ten centuries. That gap is almost incomprehensible to me when I'm barely a quarter of *one* century.

I'd get over it. I was just whining, an unappreciative spawn who was bored. Then I was too nervous to face Rafe's mother. By the time I was ready to get over myself, I heard something I wasn't supposed to, and now I don't know *what* to do.

A second prophecy. You have got to be kidding me!

Part of me wanted to march into our home, confront my parents, and demand they tell me what they were talking about. I couldn't, though. The moment Mom mentioned the doppelseers, then Dad pointed out that I can be as hardheaded and stubborn and contrary as Mom… I was already dashing away, clutching my skirts, Binx scampering right behind me as I beat a quick retreat.

It's been years since I was in the company of the doppelseers. The only twin demons in all of Sombra, they make the tiny hairs on the back of my neck stand on end. They not only have the power to see the future and utter prophecies, but they're the oldest demons in our realm.

They're the seers that saw my birth, who saw that Duke Haures would one day be bonded to a human female, and who saw that after Duchess Susanna cast the matefinder spell that cracked open the rift between Earth and Sombra, there would be many more human women who would follow… and the first one who gave birth to a half-human, half-demon spawn would bring into the world the child destined to save it.

It was Damien who uttered the fateful words more than two millennia ago:

a child born of two worlds,

belonging in both, belonging in none,
will bring with them the rain,
and the fires of Sombra will be forever done.

For my entire existence, I've felt the weight of the first two lines of the prophecy. By being both Sombran and human, I was born of two worlds, but I don't really feel like I belong in either. Sombra is my home, of course, but each of us halflings has never been able to forget that we're different than the full-blooded demons in our village, despite how much they've welcomed us and our human mothers.

And I did bring the rain. When I was only four months old, I cried as most spawn do, and the rain came. Water falling from the sky, something that's commonplace in my mother's world but unheard of in my father's, it nearly snuffed out Sombra's fires—until I was captured by King Yelios.

I didn't *do* anything. I survived him. It was Mom who found me and confronted the mad king, and Duke Haures—who, along with being the ruler of Sombra, is also a bondmaster—is the one that used the ashbalm flower to sever any ties that I might've had with Queen Alana's mate.

That's it. I didn't die. I made the rain fall with my tears, and when King Yelios was finally defeated, I became a symbol for a new age in Sombra. Even Mom admits that the first prophecy was more about the first halfling spawn setting off King Yelios's madness and his desire to take Sombra down with him, but I've gotten all the credit since.

And now there's a *second* prophecy?

Her broken wings will only end the curse when her own heart stops…

I don't know what that means, but anything that involves curses and my heart stopping—which obviously means the end of my existence or, you know, *death*—can't be good.

No wonder Mom made me promise not to go to Noctavara until I was ready. If Damien saw my future death and mentioned Noctavara, it makes sense that the fiery realm be closed off to me.

I'd never even heard of it until two gold moons ago when Katrin mentioned a squad of fire demon soldiers had visited Brille Rouge, searching for… something. She had hidden with her fellow seamstresses, so she wasn't sure *what* they were searching for, though Rafe insisted that we go to their realm and see for ourselves.

Only I couldn't break through. It was the first realm that wouldn't open to me, and I've been harboring a grudge about it ever since.

Maybe this is why. Maybe, like Mom said, I wasn't ready. Because she… she'd heard of Noctavara before. I could see it in the lines forming on her normally smooth forehead and how her dim eyes shadowed over to hear me mention the fire demon realm.

Because of the prophecy? Well, yeah, Alana. Of course it's about another prophecy.

I don't want to know. That's what I tell myself as I flee to the edge of the shadows at the end of Sombra. These same shadows were the ones that took me when I was a child, and though King Yelios no longer lurks in their depths, no one in the village will think to find me there.

Even Binx is hesitant to step paw into the shadows. Many ungez make their home in the darkest part of the woods—including Binx once—but they are the smallest and gentlest of shadow beasts. With my luck, I'll go to think… to *sulk*… and find an arkoda roaring at me for invading their territory.

And while arkodaskin makes excellent leather, it usually takes a pair of hunters to defeat the monstrous beast—and that's nothing compared to some of the fiercer creatures waiting to snack on unsuspecting demonesses.

I'm upset, but I'm not an idiot, and I don't go too far into the shadows. Just enough where I can sink down into the ash, ignoring the scattered bones lurking in the debris, as Binx curls up around my shoulders.

Then I berate myself for running. A mature demoness would have confronted Mom and Dad. If I'm in danger, hiding it from me won't help anyone, and it's not like I can stop the future from happening anyway.

If the doppelseers saw it, it'll happen. It's only a matter of when, and considering it took two thousand years for their vision of a halfling babe and a rain in Sombra to come true, there's no reason for me to be panicking now.

I give myself some time to calm down. When Binx chitters softly, telling me that I need to be heading back, I listen to my soul-pet. Besides, I need to talk to Mom. I need to ask Dad what's going on because, odds are, she won't want to tell me.

I need to—

Shit.

Rafe.

I can't believe I forgot him.

Really, Alana? What were you thinking?

I had meant to grab something to snack on from the icebox, then return to Brille Rouge to retrieve Rafe. Unfortunately, I got distracted by what I overheard, and I spent way too long in the shadows, trying to work up the nerve to confront Mom and Dad with what I did hear.

Rafe can't come back on his own. He has Loki's mage blood, but he hasn't learned the spells for portal travel yet; probably because his mother insisted that her mate not teach it to him so that she can keep a closer eye on him. If he was bonded to Katrin, he'd be able to open a path from her realm to his, but for now, it's harmless flirting and gentle wooing. Until I grab him, he's stuck in Brille Rouge.

Great. When he shows up late, Kennedy will have

a real reason to blame me. And I know I shouldn't be wary of a human woman who is a head shorter than me, but she has Freya. Even if she won't scold me, she has her ungez lecture mine.

I snap my fingers, catching Binx's attention.

He chirps, a questioning sound.

"I have to get Rafe. Want to come along?"

Despite Binx being my soul-pet, he doesn't follow me constantly; not the way the butterflies do. More often than not, he prefers to stay at home, making himself a nest on the couch, snoozing the day away. When he's in the mood for adventure, he'll take his perch on my shoulder and join us on our travels, but I never assume he wants to come.

Today he does. Probably because he can still tell that I'm shaken from what I overheard, but instead of hopping down and scampering back to Nuit, he digs his claws into the top of my dress, waiting for me to call up a portal.

I've gone to Brille Rouge so many times, it's almost instinctive. Holding up my hand, I call the shadows near my boots to me. Within seconds, there's a large rectangle shape woven of impenetrably black shadows, even darker than the patch I'm in.

Focusing on Brille Rouge, one of the realms touching ours, I step forward. As soon as my boot hits the ground again, I see the deep purple sky and glittering silver moon and know I've arrived.

That, plus the familiar voice tinged in the accent

that tells me she's speaking Brilliant calling out to me—

"Alana, thank the gods you're here. You have to help Rafe!"

I spin around so quickly, Binx's claws tear into my skin as he moves with me. I ignore it as I see the terrified look on Katrin's face.

A demoness born on this plane, she has dark brown skin, pretty pink eyes, and soft blue curls that bounce around her spiral horns. They're at least six inches long, shockingly white, and pointed at the end in a way that her ears are not.

Her eyes are huge, and as I frown, they fill with tears.

I don't see Rafe. Looking past her, there are at least four other seamstresses with the same Brilliant coloring as Katrin, but I don't see a red-skinned, fair-haired, purple-eyed halfling from Sombra anywhere.

"Rafe?" I echo. "I don't see... where is he?"

"They took him. The fire demons took him!"

"Fire demons?"

"The ones from Noctavara."

Noctavara. Of course it has to be Noctavara.

I have to separate Katrin from the other demonesses to get the story of what happened. Through soft sobs and frantic breaths, she tells me how another cadre of fire demons appeared walking down the path that leads to the building where the local seamstresses gather to weave fabric and create coverings for the inhabitants of Brille Rouge.

While Sombra is heavily male, Brille Rouge is nearly all demonesses. It isn't unusual for demons to find their way to this world, searching for mates, but the last time the fire demons had arrived, they seemed to be looking for something else.

This time, though, they decided they would gather up three of the seamstresses to bring to Noctavara with them—including Katrin. As soon as Rafe realized they were threatening the demoness he was wooing, he used his unique gift to build a protective shadow barrier around the females.

Unfortunately for Rafe, he assumed he was safe. The fire demons had come for females, and now that Katrin and her kin were out of the soldiers' reach, he believed they would move on or return to Noctavara.

And they did… but not before the soldiers surrounded Rafe, dragging him through the portal with them.

Rafe's *gone*.

What makes it even worse is that I could've saved him. Katrin confessed that the fire demons had left with Rafe mere moments before I arrived, intent on taking him back to Sombra. If I hadn't spent so long hiding in the shadows, dwelling on what I overheard, he wouldn't have been in Brille Rouge to be caught.

Does that mean that the demonesses might've been captured instead? Probably, but while I think Katrin is nice enough, it's Rafe I'm worried about.

He's in Noctavara. The same realm that features in the second prophecy I way-too-coincidentally only heard mentioned for the first time today—and the world that refused to allow me entry the first time I tried.

I have to try again. There's no other choice. This is my fault. No matter what happens to me if I visit Noctavara, it doesn't matter. I promised Rafe that I'd return for him and bring him home. That might just take a little longer, but I'm determined.

If fire demons brought my friend to another world, I'm going to go and bring him back.

That's what I tell Katrin. She seems relieved, as though grateful that she can pass the responsibility of worrying about Rafe's abduction to me instead of it weighing down her shoulders. I know then that she was only playing with Rafe's attention. She was never going to offer him her essence or take him as her bonded mate. If she were, she'd insist on joining me on the trip to Noctavara.

Assuming my shadows will work this time, that is.

I ask her to tell me the direction that the soldiers came from, hoping they left enough of a trace of their portal that I can use my shadows to break through it. And, okay, maybe I didn't want an audience in case Noctavara blocked me again. After a dainty point of her fingers, I set off with Binx, not even surprised when Katrin and the remaining seamstresses all flee into the structure behind them as though ready to hide.

If only I could. But, no… I did my hiding already today. What did that get me? My best friend is missing —and I'm going to do whatever it takes to get him back.

OH, I SHOULDN'T BE DOING THIS.

Though I'm determined as ever to rescue Rafe, the thought repeats as I stand at the edge of the road, shadows pooling restlessly around my boots like they're waiting for permission I haven't quite given them yet. Binx is still perched on my shoulder, his small body warm against my neck, his tail flicking in quick, agitated swishes that mirror my own unease.

Rafe is gone. I knew that, but I don't think I really *understood* what Katrin told me until I'm standing alone, prepared to follow my friend into a realm that obviously doesn't want me. Rafe is gone, and there's no one I can blame but myself (and, well, the fire demons, but other than that, it's all my fault).

I should have stayed by his side when he was flirting with Katrin instead of leaving him behind to sulk in Sombra. I should have returned when I said I would instead of figuring that he'd appreciate more time with his demoness before he had to answer to Kennedy and Loki.

I should've warned him not to get involved with Noctavara after the last time the fire demons arrived in Brille Rouge and we were unable to sate our curiosity by following them to their world.

Noctavara.

Of course it has to be Noctavara.

We can't let her go to Noctavara…

I hadn't stayed long enough to hear the rest. I hadn't needed to, and, whoa, am I regretting that now.

That's something else that's my fault. I should be used to it, though. Prophecies have ruled my life since before I could hold my head up on my own. Four months old and already chosen. Now it's twenty-five years later, and I'm still treated like a wonder instead of a person. Even worse, right when I learn there's a second prophecy that might lead to the *end* of my life, it looks like my trip to Noctavara might be happening sooner than later.

We can't let her go to Noctavara…

Sorry, Mom. I… I have to.

"If this is Fate," I mutter, staring at the space in front of me that's as good as any other, "it has a sick sense of timing."

Binx chitters softly, a sound that vibrates through my bones, grounding me. He knows what I'm trying to do. He also knows it isn't working.

Because it isn't.

My gift is instinctive. I draw the shadows in, direct them with my palm, and imagine where I want to go. Deep down, I feel a catch as the shadows answer me immediately. They're eager and familiar. They're *alive*. I shape them the way I always do, feeling for the thin place between worlds. I picture the seam opening, the dark folding back on itself, the path to Noctavara opening, and… yeah.

Nothing happens.

I try again.

Harder this time. My heart stutters, a warning echoing in my chest that feels uncomfortably like my mother's voice telling me to stop. To go home. To only venture into Noctavara when I'm ready.

I'm not ready. To face my fate, or to find out what the doppelseers have in store for me. But Rafe is missing, and the only clue that I have is that soldiers from Noctavara stole him.

I have to get in there. I *have* to.

I flex my fingers. I grit my teeth. I gnash my baby fangs, stamping my boots on soft earth.

Still nothing.

I'm blocked.

The realization makes my guts twist into knots. "No," I snap, angry and worried and afraid. "You don't get to keep me out."

My shadows recoil, stunned yet endlessly obedient, waiting for me to try again. My panicked breath comes faster, panic clawing at the edges of my resolve.

Rafe is out there. Alone. Taken because he protected someone else. Taken because I wasn't there to protect *him*.

And I'm stuck on the other side of the veil, unable to reach him.

Binx crawls higher, pressing his small forehead beneath my chin. That helps. Having my soul-pet with me always helps me calm down, and as he chirps gently, I shudder out a breath.

"I'm going," I tell him. "If you'd rather I take you to Sombra first, I can. But there's no one who can go after Rafe but me."

I believe that wholeheartedly. Why? No clue. But as though something is telling me that this is it, this is the prophecy Mom mentioned beginning to unfold, I know I'm right. I have to figure out a way to go after Rafe, though I refuse to put Binx in any danger—

He makes a harsh sound.

"I know, but—"

He swishes his tail.

"Of course you can come, but—"

He nuzzles the side of my throat. I swallow the lump that suddenly lodges there.

"Okay, Binx. We go together."

He chitters softly, and I let out a soft sigh, ready to try again. That's what I'll do. I'll try and I'll try, and whatever's keeping me out will have to push forever because that's how long it'll take before I stop.

It doesn't occur to me to ask Rafe's dad for help. Loki's a mage and a whizz with travel spells, but this… this is something I have to do.

I'm lifting my hand when, suddenly, a flicker of movement catches my eye.

I turn just in time to see it drift in my path. To my stunned surprise, it's a butterfly, but so unlike the faripoz in Sombra. Instead of glowing white against the shadows, this butterfly has orange-and-black wings. They're tattered at the edges, one side nearly completely torn, making it wobble as it flaps toward me.

My breath catches.

Binx goes very still.

I've seen one of those before. One of the first paintings I remember Dad making for me was a land-scape that featured Sombra on one half of the canvas, Earth on the other. Dark shadows, fiery ash fields, dark trees, and Sombra's two moons compared to a blue human sky, green ground, and so much light.

That's not all, either. After my rescue as an infant, it became clear that the faripoz in Sombra had imprinted on me. Dad painted white butterflies on the Sombra side. On the Earth side? Butterflies in so many different shapes and sizes and colors.

Including one with orange-and-black wings.

Later, when me, Mom, and Dad took one of our trips to her world, Mom pointed out the very same butterflies passing through our mist, concealing us from the mortals. Tucked in Dad's shadows, she giggled when the butterfly landed on my nose before fluttering away.

A monarch butterfly, she called it, and one that's native to Earth.

So what is it doing in Brille Rouge?

When it lands on my outstretched fingers, the contact sends a jolt through me. My shadows surge in response, no longer unyielding as they struggle to create another portal, but pulling me somewhere.

Pulling me to Noctavara.

Because it doesn't belong in Brille Rouge, does it? It belongs in Noctavara—and, suddenly, the rift between this realm and that one is *open.*

At the same time, the ground beneath my feet darkens, shadows stretching and twisting, opening into a rippling rectangle as I finally summon another portal.

My heart hammers. Fear coils tight in my chest, but I banish it. And then I hear Mom's worried words echoing in my ears again.

Her broken wings will only end the curse when her own heart stops…

I look down at the butterfly, its broken wings trembling against my skin.

"I don't care," I tell the strange creature. "Not if it means saving him."

Binx chirps once in agreement before scrambling fully onto my shoulder, resuming his usual pose.

With one hand on his rump, I step forward.

For a heartbeat, the shadows close in around us. In the next, they're spitting us out again.

I stumble forward, boots skidding on ground that's too solid, too *real*, and barely catch myself before I would've ended up pitching face-first into the damp earth. The portal snaps shut behind me with a sound like a breath being sucked in, and the sudden silence that follows is worse than the noise in Nuit ever was.

I straighten slowly.

The air here is… different.

Katrin said they were fire demons, but Sombra is far warmer than this world. It's cool, but not cold; not like Earth. The air is thick, like it's been sitting still for centuries. Above me, the sky is caught in a perpetual twilight with a silver moon and a spattering of stars filtering through the interlaced branches over my head.

Trees surround me. Not the ash-dark giants of Sombra's shadows, but silver-barked trunks twisted in unfamiliar shapes, their leaves narrow and dark, whispering softly to one another even though there's no wind strong enough to justify the sound.

My heart rate kicks up. My shadows curl instinctively around my boots, seeking comfort. I do the same to Binx, burying my fingers through his fur.

"Alright," I murmur, forcing calm into my voice. "New world, new rules."

Binx shifts on my shoulder, his small body taut, ears twitching as he listens to things I can't hear yet. His tail flicks once, twice, uneasy, but not panicked. Not yet.

That's good.

If Binx isn't panicking, I won't either.

I take a careful step forward, looking around and, thankfully, seeing no one.

The cushioned ground gives beneath my boot with a faint, wet sound. Somewhere to my left, something scuttles away, quick and low to the ground. Farther off, a branch creaks. My quickened breath matches the sound.

The woods are not quiet. Oh, no. They're *listening*.

I swallow and move again, slower this time, every sense stretched thin. The farther I go, the more aware I become of how alone I am. No portals humming at my back. No easy escape tugging at my spine.

Rafe.

The thought of him being trapped in this spooky realm steadies me.

"I'll find you," I whisper, not caring who hears. "I promise."

A soft flutter draws my attention upward.

Tattered orange-and-black wings drift between the branches ahead, the same butterfly from before moving with lazy certainty, as if it knows exactly where it's going. And maybe it does because, as I watch it, it winks out of sight.

"Figures," I mutter.

I move closer, hoping it's just a trick of the dim light. The way I see it, the butterfly brought me here. If I'm lucky, it'll bring me to Rafe.

The woods seem to close in as I walk, trees growing next to each other, my surroundings dimming even further until the light feels filtered through smoke. My shadows trail behind me, thinner than I like, clinging instead of flowing.

That's when I hear it.

A footstep.

Not heavy. Not clumsy.

Close.

I pause.

Binx freezes, claws pricking lightly through the fabric of my dress as he lowers himself, making his ungez body smaller than usual.

The sound doesn't come again.

I turn slowly, scanning the trees, every muscle coiled tight. "Hello?" I call, keeping my tone even. Unafraid. I'm full of it, of course, but whoever's out there has no clue.

Right?

I strain my ears, but nothing happens. No one answers.

I exhale roughly, annoyed with myself for being so jumpy, and take another hesitant step, peering upward as I do, back to looking for the butterfly.

And that's when I find a sharp blade at my throat.

CHAPTER 4
THANE AUREX

In Sombra, we don't use swords. Not even Duke Haures's guard wields such a weapon. Why should they? When a demon's horns and claws cause more than enough damage in a fight, and the threat of being left to the beasts at the edge of the shadows is any even bigger one.

That doesn't mean we don't have any blades or that I don't know what they are. Clara's father, Glaine, is the head of the duke's soldiers. He has a silver sword that is known as a demon killer, given to him by Duke Haures.

Guess what it does.

Humans can die in a hundred different ways unless they have a Sombran's essence to grant them immortality. That doesn't mean someone like Mom or Dad *can't* die. They can, and one quick slash from a sword to the neck is one of the surefire ways to end their existence. I'm a halfling. I don't know what I can survive, but I'd rather not find out when Rafe is in danger and my parents have no idea where I've disappeared off to.

So I stay still. The metal is cold. It doesn't cut, not yet, and there's no blood drawn, though that can change at any moment. In fact, I feel a hum of magic through the blade, almost like it's deciding whether I'm worthy of a killing strike.

So, yes, I freeze and only hope that whoever is holding the sword decides against taking my head and my life.

"Well," a voice says pleasantly, right beside my ear as a warm body presses into my back, "you're either very brave or very stupid."

The accent is lilting, something I notice above my sudden fear because it's easier than focusing on the sharp edge of the sword. Fae. I've been to enough of their realms to recognize it. Even more interesting, over the pounding in my ears, I can understand what he said. There's usually a language barrier between realms—just like how my parents couldn't understand one another until Dad first triggered the essence exchange—though demon languages all share a base dialect that means I can usually communicate with those in Brille Rouge and Soleil, no problem.

But if I pulled this off, then I'm finally in Noctavara, and I just might have found myself in a fae realm with a fae swordsman who has his sword up against my neck.

Can't forget that part, and I don't. I still don't move, either, waiting to see what he's going to do. Then, in a voice that's meant to tell him that I'm nowhere near as terrified as I currently am, I say in Sombran, "You're standing too close for a friendly 'hello', stranger."

A soft laugh answers me. It's warm and amused, entirely unbothered by the fact that he's threatening me wordlessly. I wonder if he was able to understand my flippant reply, and can't decide if he did even as the blade slowly eases back and away from my skin.

It's not enough to feel safe, but the right amount to get my panicked heart to start beating again. With Binx standing still at my ankle, I slowly turn to face him.

Fire demon. That's what Katrin said, both the first time they came to Brille Rouge and their latest return. She insisted that it was a cadre of fire demon soldiers that attacked before dragging Rafe through a portal into their realm. His accent suggested otherwise, and one glimpse at the male watching me with uncon- cealed interest tells me I'm right.

Fae. Not demon, not human, but something else. They have their own powers, their own abilities, and their own weaknesses. After I met my first fae, I asked Mom if we had any books about them in the EL. She'd snickered, mentioning the romance section, but

Kennedy took pity on me. A mage himself, Loki retrieved a small book for me from the School of Mages that spoke of the few fae realms that Sombra had contact with over the ages.

Noctavara wasn't in there—and after the first time I realized it was blocked to me, I checked again—but Arcadia and the island of Tir na nÓg were. Realms that were ruled by their king or queen, with a court-like structure and people who could glamour and charm, though they were unable to tell a lie. They had no interest in a relationship with Sombra, though that could be because King Yelios and my namesake, Queen Alana, attempted to invade Arcadia during their reign thousands of years ago. Most demons think it was just other demon realms they wanted to take over, but according to the book Loki let me borrow, they tried to go after neighboring demon realms, fae realms, even a world full of djinn before Queen Alana perished and King Yelios lost his mind.

No wonder Duke Haures decided to close Sombra off to most realms—until a silly halfling shadow walker decided to use her power to break out of Nuit…

My first instinct now that I'm not in danger of being skewered like a piece of meat is to gather my shadows and rip open a portal that will bring Binx and me back to Sombra. I try. It doesn't work. Just like how I struggled to reach Noctavara until the Earth butterfly landed on my finger, I'm blocked.

I'm blocked, and I can feel the weight of the fae's curious stare on me as I flex my fingers at my side and nothing happens. Figuring I have no other choice, I glance up at him and, yup, there I go again.

I'm *stunned*.

He's leaning against a silver-barked tree like he's been waiting there for me to see him all night, posture loose, attention razor-sharp. Dark curls fall forward into his amber-colored eyes, catching faint traces of moonlight peeking down on us from the dark sky over our heads. His grin is wicked yet also easy, the kind that belongs to someone who knows exactly how dangerous he is.

The hilt of his short sword rests easily in his hand like an extension of himself. As I peer at it, his grin widens into a joking smile as he slips it into the sheath at his waist. Like the rest of his coverings, it's dark, swallowing up the glimmering silver blade. I'm half-shadow demon, yet he's the one who could easily melt into the black of this forest. Well, except for the obvious golden gleam of his fae skin, warring with the strength of the full moon's glow.

No wonder Katrin believed his people were fire demons. My first impression of him is of heat, of a glow that breaks through the dark, shadowy forest, and a sensation that I'm burning up from the inside out. As I stare at him, everything in me tightens as I take in the dark-haired, amber-eyed, pointy-eared stranger who, suddenly, doesn't feel like much of one at all…

"And you," he says, gaze sliding over me with open interest as he keeps his pose lazy despite the way he seems almost surprised to have found me in his woods, "are not supposed to be here."

"That makes two of us," I toss back before I think better of it. It's like the words slip out, similar to how Binx keeps making a soft, warning sound somewhere near the dark ground beneath us. It's harder than I'm used to, nothing like the ash of Sombra, but more like the solid floor you find on Earth with only a hint of something covering it.

Grass, I remember. That's what Mom called the green plants growing on the hard earth of her home realm. Noctavara has something similar, something that cushions the ground and keeps my boots from digging deeper as I take a careful step closer to my ungez.

The fae male's smile deepens now, both slow and knowing. "Oh, I'm exactly where I'm supposed to be."

He's not speaking Sombran. That much is obvious. I'd know those harsh, grating syllables anywhere, and the clipped words that are Mom's human language are nowhere as beautiful as the lyrical-sounding sentences he's been uttering. Still, I can understand him, and he can understand me, and as long as he keeps that sword hidden, that's the last thing I need to worry about until I can open the portal, grab Binx, and come up with a plan B to save Rafe.

And maybe I was letting my guard down too quickly because, out of nowhere, Binx lunges up and hurries forward, heading toward the male. Shadows ripple over the ungez's sleek form, his white eyes glowing softly in the dim light. He pauses near the fae's boots, fluffy tail flicking once as his ears twitch.

The fae's attention snaps downward.

"Well," he murmurs, crouching slightly, fascination cutting through his amusement. "You're new."

Binx stares at him, unblinking.

"Careful," I say, staying back though everything in me wants to surge forward myself and swoop Binx up to safety in my arms. There's no need. I know that. Binx can take care of himself, and remembering how my soul-pet has shown his annoyance with Rafe more than once, I tack on helpfully, "He bites."

That earns me a laugh. A real one as, for the first time, his eyes lock on mine.

Oh, he was looking me over before, but almost as though he was avoiding direct eye contact, our gazes never met… until now.

If I thought looking at him was a gut punch before, that's nothing compared to the tremor that runs through me when I look directly into his eyes. My fingers flex again, of their own accord this go-round, and my tongue suddenly feels too big to be in my mouth. I tremble, my claws growing, my belly twisting.

My heart skips a beat. I swear, for a moment there, it nearly stops, and I suddenly—*suddenly*—understand what Stevie meant when she told me that she just knew that Corbin was her fated mate.

Why? Because I'm looking at mine.

This fae male, whoever he is, is my one true mate, and the way his expression doesn't change at all, his long, slender, golden fingers hovering outstretched toward Binx as he glances at me before looking down at my soul-pet… he has no idea that I recognize him as mine.

If he's mine, that means I'm his. That's how mate bonds work. Though, I have to admit, not every fated pair has the ability to recognize each other. Humans can't sense a bond until their demon mate gives them their essence. Is it the same for fae?

I don't know, and I realize that that's one detail that the fae book I read forgot to mention. Probably because it doesn't seem like fae and demons mate very often, but if he's mine, then the gods have a wicked sense of humor considering how my supposed mate greeted me with a sword to my neck.

Should I tell him? I open my mouth to say something, *anything*, when Binx jumps up, sinking his fangs into the fae's finger.

For a second, I stare, watching the shock flicker across the fae's sculpted features as Binx hangs on tight. The fae rises up to his full height. Binx still hasn't let go. This time, I do hurry forward. Mate or not, I don't know this male. I don't trust him. If he tries to hurt Binx, I'll have to stop him.

Instead of shaking his hand to get the ungez to release him, he just arches his eyebrows and waits for Binx to stop biting him. Once I bury my fingers through the edges of Binx's shadows, my soul-pet recognizes me. He relaxes his tiny jaw so that I can lift him up and off of the fae.

Two puncture wounds cover the top of his finger. Glittery blood wells up there, and since he seems more surprised by the bite than angry, I can't help but say, "Told you so."

He cocks his head. "So you did."

CHAPTER 5

TRAPPED

I watch as he lifts his finger to his mouth, tongue dabbing at the blood. By the time he's done, the wounds are already healing, and I've gotten a good peek at the tiny canine fangs barely peeking past his bottom lip as he gives Binx a curious once-over.

"I thought the beast was made of shadow," he muses. "His bite was nothing less than solid."

"That's because he's a Sombra beast," I find myself compelled to explain regardless. "He's part shadow, part living creature. If you touch past the edge of his shadows, he's as firm as you and me."

I tested that, too. While I can turn to mist in Mom's human world, just like when I'm in Sombra, I'm trapped in a solid shape with my shadows barely reacting to my call. It's like they've been tamed, the magic out of my reach. I can't create a portal or disappear into their darkness... I'm trapped in this realm in more ways than one, and I have no idea what I'm going to do about that.

First, find Rafe. Second, figure out why my essence is telling me that this fae male is mine. Third, make my shadows listen to me again. Who knows? Maybe they're just exhausted from how I pushed them to let me into this realm. Once I'm ready to leave again, they should work.

Right?

I have to believe that. Just like I have to believe that the gods have some kind of grand plan in mind for me that doesn't end with me finding my one true mate, then losing him—and my life—in this unfamiliar realm…

As I think, I can't help but watch him. He's watching me, too, a sudden silence stretching between us, thick with so many things unspoken. Like, oh, how he's my mate, and how he must be wondering who *I* am and how I came to be in Noctavara if it really is supposed to closed-off to travelers.

That's why I don't just turn and walk away. Not because I'm finding it difficult to resist the fledgling bond that sprang up between us the second I looked in his eyes and *knew* he was mine, but because I need some kind of sign that he feels it, too… or that he doesn't.

Does he?

The fae male's bright eyes dart over my face, taking

in my golden peepers and how—thanks to Dad's demon side—they glow as notably as his skin does. His eyes don't light up like mine, and if I chose to, I could dampen the glow until they're as dead as Mom's blue eyes, but while their shine doesn't seem to interest him that much, it's the inch-long black horns attached to my forehead that have him frowning as he notices them.

I don't like the way he's scrutinizing me. Shifting Binx so that the ungez is resting on my shoulder, his fluffy tail wrapped around the back of my neck, I beat a quick retreat in case he remembers he has a sword and uses it on him.

Only it's not Binx he's paying close attention to. Instead, his gaze follows my retreat before he gestures at my hairline. "From the look of those, I'm thinking you don't have any coin I can convince you to part with."

Pausing when there's at least a demon's length between us, I run my fingers over my right horn. That's right. Like my human mother, he doesn't have any horns. I don't see how that has anything to do with my having… what was that word again?

"Coin?" I echo.

"Gold?" he suggests.

Gold is a color. Like my eyes, and his deliciously tempting skin… I don't have to be the daughter of our clan's artist to know that. In Sombra, we have the gold moon that arrives and brings fertility with it, and golden chains that the mages conjure for Duke Haures's prisoners.

I shake my head.

"Money?"

Oh. That's what he's asking me about?

"We don't have money in Nuit. We trade for what we need from the rest of our clan." I pause for a moment. *Convince you to part with…* with the help of a sword, huh? "You're a thief?"

The fae male grins at me. "In the Shadowed Woods of the Gilded Court, we prefer the term 'bandit'."

My brow furrows. "This is supposed to be Noctavara."

Isn't it?

"Yes. But the Gilded Court rules the realm, with the Shadowed Woods being only a part of it." His fingers tap the hilt of his sword, drawing my attention. "And, like I said before, you're not supposed to be here. But since you are…"

Maybe I'm not, but that's not going to stop me. "Is it forbidden?"

In Sombra, it's forbidden for humans to learn about demons. I have no idea what to expect from Noctavara, especially now that my essence is telling me that a fae thief—oh, sorry, *bandit*—is my one true mate. All the more reason not to tell him so, especially when my focus is on finding Rafe.

Which might be easier said than done if I'm not allowed to be here…

He blinks, his easy humor fading. "Forbidden? Now, why would you say that?"

I shrug. "I have my reasons for visiting this realm. If I can expect others like you to greet me at sword-point, I should know so that I can expect it."

"In the Shadowed Woods, you can almost guarantee it—"

Wonderful.

"—and those aren't the worst of the dangers here. What about your shadows? You're from Sombra, yes? Can't they protect you? Don't you have shadow magic of your own?"

How does he know about Sombra, I wonder. Unless Rafe isn't the first one of my kind that's been captured by soldiers from this world… "Have you met another Sombra demon before?"

If the fae notices that I'm being as careful with my words as he's been, he doesn't show it.

"All sorts pass through the Shadowed Woods," is his answer. Leaning back against the tree again, he adds, "But they're usually accompanied by members of the Gilded Court."

That's the second time he's mentioned the Gilded Court. Hmm… "So if I was searching for someone, that's where I should go? Who I should go see?"

"Should you? No. But everyone in Noctavara is brought before Queen Celeste sooner or later."

I don't care about a queen. I just want to find out who took Rafe. Anything else can wait. "Thank you—"

He winces.

Binx claws at my shoulder, as though making sure I saw that. Since I did, I ask, "Something wrong?"

"You're not fae."

I'm not, and I shake my head. He already saw the horns that are a dead giveaway to my demon heritage, and he seems to know something about Sombra. "No."

"Don't thank the fae," he tells me, his voice full of amusement while his expression is anything but. "Unless you want to owe us a debt. And there are many of us in Noctavara who want more than gold…"

The way he lets his sentence trail off, it's as though he's waiting for me to finally introduce myself. I can't believe I haven't already. Mom would cluck her tongue at my lack of manners if she were here. Maybe if I'd run off once he took the sword away from my throat, he wouldn't need to learn my name, but I've lingered despite knowing I shouldn't—and all because I can't bring myself to walk away just yet.

He's my mate. My *mate*. He won't let me thank him for the information he's shared so far, but the least I can do is give him my name. "Alana," I supply. "Of Sombra."

This time, the humor reaches his eyes—or maybe

that's a sense of satisfaction I can't deny. "You may call me Thane. Thane Aurex."

Thane. I roll the name around my head. *Thane*. It suits him.

"You're lucky you found me, Alana of Sombra. Or that I found you. There isn't another bandit in the Shadowed Woods who might be willing to help you find your way out of it."

Is that so? Then why is he offering? Could it be that he *does* sense the mate bond the same way that I do?

"Why? I don't have any gold," I remind him. "Why would you be willing to help me?"

"Because you'll never be able to do it on your own."

Huh. Is *that* so?

Later, I'll admit that allowing the easy way that Thane dismissed me to make me upset was a mistake. He was right. I'm in a world I don't know, with no solid leads to track down my best friend, and a forest unlike the shadows I grew up around surrounding me. My powers are failing, Binx is nudging me to figure out how to return to Sombra so we can get help, and a cocky fae is looking at me as though I'll up and swoon and act like I'm some damsel in distress so he can be the hero in one of the romance books Mom stocks in the EL.

So I'm undeniably attracted to him. So my instincts are telling me that he's supposed to be my mate. If he *is* my mate, he'll learn sooner or later that you don't tell Alana of Sombra what she can and cannot do.

Binx knows. He digs his shadow claws into the fabric of my dress while I grab my skirts, ready to walk away.

And that's when, over Thane's shoulders, I see another one of the orange-and-black butterflies. It's not the same as the one that led me into Noctavara, but that doesn't matter. If a monarch butterfly helped me arrive in the fae realm, maybe it's all I need to track down Rafe.

Thane never expected me to run. Maybe fae women don't, and there are plenty of demonesses in Nuit who might sniff in distaste if I did so in the village square, but as the butterfly continues to flap behind Thane, then beyond him, I don't hesitate.

His eyes widen, though he must not think I'm any sort of threat because he leaves his sword hanging at his side as Binx and I dash right past him. He realizes too late that I wasn't moving toward him, reaching out to snag my arm after I've already made it by his side.

His voice chases me, though he doesn't.

"Where are you going?"

"I'm following the butterfly!"

"What? No! Don't—"

Too late, Thane. I'm already running after it, and if part of me hopes that the fae male might feel a pull toward me and suddenly realize that I'm supposed to be *his* mate, the guilt over abandoning Rafe is definitely stronger than my libido.

For now. When the it's time for the gold moon back home, I'll find it harder to resist the pull I feel toward him, but I have plenty of moons until then. Until then, I need a plan.

Okay, Alana. Let's go.

Step one: follow the butterfly, find Rafe, and rescue him from the Noctavaran soldiers who took him before the gold moon rises in Sombra.

Step two: show Thane that I can do anything if I put my mind to it, and maybe see if he knows anything about a demon mate bond or how to initiate —or block—an essence exchange before we're stuck with each other forever.

Step three—

Godsdamn it, I never even make it to step one. Not yet, at least. Too consumed with chasing after the butterfly while also keeping an ear out, listening for some sign that Thane is following us, I don't pay attention to my surroundings. I just keep running, one hand on Binx's rump so that I don't lose my ungez, until the monarch butterfly suddenly winks out of existence.

I dig my feet into the too-hard ground, spinning around wildly, swallowing some of Mom's most creative curses as I realize that I'm alone in another clearing that's surrounded by shadow-dark trees without any clue where to go next.

I walk around, looking up, my head swiveling back and forth, frustrated and alone, when something snags around the ankle of my arkodaskin boot. It catches, going tight, and before I can revise how I should approach step one, the world flips upside down.

Or maybe that's just me.

Very brave or very stupid, huh? Guess which one I am.

So... I'm trapped.

My claws aren't sharp enough to cut through the twine that's wrapped around my ankle, keeping me flipped over as I sway about three feet off of the ground. As a halfling, I can't shift to shadows so that I can escape its hold on me, either, even when I have better control on my magic.

And that's not the worst part.

These days, it's the fashion in Sombra to wear undercoverings woven from shadows. It's something our human mothers brought with them from their world, calling them 'panties', only instead of the panties being made from fabric like my dresses, they're shadow. If I had any doubt that my magic was somehow being blocked now that I'm in Noctavara, the slight breeze blowing against my lower half makes it clear. My shadow panties are *gone*.

Building some momentum, I swing back and forth just to check. My skirts have fallen, tangling around the bodice of my dress. I clamp my arms to my side and, on an upswing, I peek, groaning softly when I see the pale curls instead of the shadow coverings.

Great. Just great. I'm hanging upside down, my cunt on display... this is not how I planned on making a good impression on my one true mate.

Hopefully he doesn't change his mind and follow after me. I'd barely left Thane in the other clearing before I found myself in trouble. Good going, Alana. I wanted to prove that I didn't need his help, that I could do this on my own, only to end up in a snare trap as Binx paces beneath me.

Leaping up, my soul-pet bats at my hair. I close my eyes and wonder how long I'll be hanging here before one of those bandits that Thane mentioned finds me. Or a hunter. It could happen. I know that Nuit has more than a few in our village, each one using traps like these to catch the larger shadow beasts to provide meat for the clan.

Before I was born, the hunters used to catch ungez. After Kennedy's soul-pet, Freya, proved how useful they can be when they bond to a human, a demon, or a halfling, Duke Haures decreed that they no longer be caught and cooked. I couldn't imagine eating something as adorable and personable as Binx, but considering the trap was set for prey as big as a halfling, I'd hate to see what the hunters were expecting—or what they'll do when they find me in their trap.

No. I have to get down. I have to—

There isn't even enough time for me to scream. Out of the corner of my eye, I see movement in the shadows behind me. There's a rustling sound, then a whistle, and I'm *falling*—

"Oof."

Someone catches me. I was almost sure that I was going to land on my face. Luckily, that doesn't happen. Before I know it, there's an arm around my back, one tucked under my knees, and my savior shifts my body so that I'm cradled against their chest instead of hitting the ground with my head.

I look at them. No wonder I couldn't see who it was. A deep black cloak—like shadows, but made of an impossibly dark fabric instead—covers my rescuer from head to toe. Even their hands are hidden by the cloak. It doesn't matter. My heart trips to have him near again, almost as though my body recognizes his even when my eyes can't see him.

Reaching up, I find the seam where his cloak folds in on itself, hiding his face. If all of the bandits wear cloaks like this, it explains how Thane was able to sneak up on me with his sword in the first place, and how he was able to cut me down from the snare trap that had me hanging from the tree before I knew he was there.

That must be what happened. Because, as I push back his hood, his eyes seem to dance with laughter as I reveal his face.

"Thane," I breathe out. "You're fast." I think about how he snatched me from the air, holding me easily as though I weigh nothing at all. "You're strong."

He shrugs. "I'm fae."

So he is.

And I'm in big, big trouble.

I clear my throat. "Than—" Nope. Don't thank the fae. "I appreciate your help, but if you could put me down…"

Without a word, he tilts me so that I can stand on my boots before reaching down, smoothing my skirts until I'm fully covered again. Avoiding Thane's gaze, I see Binx rising up on his back legs, forelegs folded in front of him as his nose twitches. Right next to my ungez is Thane's silver sword. Just like I thought, he probably pulled his sword to cut me down, dropped it to catch me.

I just wish I knew why.

I wish I could understand *anything* about this male.

Just… not enough to trigger an essence exchange before I'm one hundred percent certain I want to keep him as my mate. Since I'm not, I keep my hands to myself, putting a few steps between us as I wonder why he came after me.

CHAPTER 6

TELL THEM THAT I'M COMING

There's a pause as I ask myself whether or not I should ask him that. The woods hum around us, quiet yet watchful. I have the feeling that someone—or some*thing*—is lurking near, and as though Thane agrees, he bends quickly, his cloak fanning out behind him. Grabbing his sword, he gives it a quick looksie before putting it back in its sheath.

Straightening again, Thane's expression shifts. It's not the easy smile he seems to flash habitually. Not the bandit's charm from before, either. Oh, no. This is something different, something that has me on edge as I rub my fingers together, a wordless signal to my soul-pet.

Binx scampers up my skirts, darting around my front. Once he hits my shoulder, he resumes his perch, growling softly at the fae.

Thane raises his eyebrows at me. "So you followed the butterfly," he says.

It's not a question. It's a gentle rebuke, and he reminds me of the way my mother begins a conversation before she lectures me.

I react the same way: I stiffen. "It was there, and I thought—"

"They usually are," he replies, cutting me off. His gaze flicks over to the monarch butterfly drifting lazily nearby that seems to have appeared out of nowhere again. Its wings almost shimmer beneath the moonlight. "That doesn't mean you should chase them. Not when you don't know how dangerous the Shadowed Woods can be."

Part of me wants to tell Thane that I was raised in Nuit, a village at the edge of the shadows. When I was four months old, I was abducted and hidden in the shadows on the orders of a mad demon king. The glowing white butterflies in Sombra have always protected me, and the monarch butterflies brought me here in the first place. So I got caught in the snare trap. I'm sure, between Binx and me, I would've gotten down… eventually.

I scowl. My shadows still aren't thickening enough that I feel confident I can create a portal, but my annoyance has them flickering around my boots. Binx rubs his fluffy cheek against mine. The orange-and-black winged butterfly flaps closer, settling on my right horn.

Thane's lips come together, not quite a frown but almost. "I see."

I shake my head. The butterfly flutters upward, then nestles on the top of my hair. I leave it, and when Binx lifts a paw, prepared to stretch up and bat the nearest wing, I murmur 'no' under my breath.

Thane moves easily, gracefully, coming to stand at my other side, amber eyes taking in the butterfly crown.

"You followed the queen's butterflies," he points out. "From your realm, too?"

From Brille Rouge, actually, but he doesn't need to know the details. And queen's butterflies… that must be how he refers to the monarch butterflies in his fae language, and how I'm somehow translating it. "Yes."

His head tilts slightly. "I wonder why you would. What are you doing in Noctavara? The butterflies invited you, but you came. Humor me, Alana of Sombra. Why are you here?"

Should I tell him? My brain says I shouldn't. My heart—my *essence*—says that I shouldn't hide this from my mate. My gut says I should tell him the truth and see how he reacts to—

"Rafe," I admit, ignoring how Binx is chittering again, my soul-pet warning me against trusting the fae bandit too quickly. "I'm here because your soldiers took him from me, and I'm going to get him back."

Another swish. Another move. Suddenly, Thane is on my other side, staring at my profile. "Your lover?"

Lover? I scoff out a laugh, even if I'm secretly pleased that Thane would come to that conclusion. Sure, he sounds more curious than jealous, but that's better than him not caring at all.

"No," I tell him. "Rafe is… he's like my kin. A brother to me. He's Sombran, too, but he was visiting a different demon realm when soldiers from this world stole him. They'd come for a clan of demonesses, but he protected them with a shadow barrier, leaving him to be the only one dragged into Noctavara."

That I know of, I should say. I only hope that, once Rafe was in this world, the soldiers didn't go back for Katrin and her fellow seamstresses.

"So he has shadow magic?" asks Thane. "This Rafe of yours?"

"Sombra is a world of shadows. If you're part demon or demoness, we all do to some degree. It's how we survive."

"And that's how you made it to Noctavara."

"Only because the butterflies opened the path for me," I remind him, nodding to draw his attention to the butterfly that hasn't left my hair yet. "Is that how you found me just now?"

In Nuit, all anyone had to do was follow the glowing white butterflies to track me down. And now, in Noctavara, it seems like it's these strange Earth butterflies that keep appearing—

"No."

Oh. *Wait.* It's the bond, isn't it? He *knows*—

"I didn't have to follow the queen's butterflies when I know the Shadowed Woods better than anyone," explains Thane. "I knew which way you ran off to. I know the traps."

I perch my hands on my hips. "You're the reason I was hanging upside down like that?"

"I said I know the traps, Alana, not that I'm responsible for all of them. At least, not the one that had your skirts down by your ears."

Because that's so much better. And I really needed that reminder that he very well could've seen my cunt and my rear before he cut me down…

"So there's more," I'm guessing. "Traps, that is."

"Plenty."

Great.

"That's why, if you stay with me," he adds, his lilt almost seductive in his promise, "I'll guarantee you'll make it to the Court alive."

Stay with him? Where did that come from? "Why would I do that?"

I wait for him to tell me that I'm his mate so of course I have to stay with him. If not that, then he'll explain why a fae bandit who can't rob me of the gold I don't have is interested in… what? Helping me?

And the Court? Why does he think I'm going to the Court? He mentioned it before, implying that Rafe might end up there, but what if I could find my friend before he gets into any further trouble?

I get the answer to that last one first.

"It's very simple. If the soldiers retrieved your Rafe from a demon realm, they brought him to Noctavara for one purpose only. They'll pass him on to either one of the nobles in the Gilded Court or sell him to wandering slavers at their first opportune moment."

I gulp. "Slavers?"

Thane nods. "I mentioned them before. Odds are they were slavers who took him in the first place. Soldiers are usually stationed throughout Noctavara. They wouldn't dare risk the queen's wrath by leaving. But slavers… they would, and they'd be forgiven if they brought their finds to the queen."

"Is that what they'll do with Rafe?"

"It's fair to say. Sooner or later, everyone goes before Queen Celeste as she reigns over the Gilded Court, whether they're in chains or not. For him to build a shadow barrier… I know you said it isn't you, but does he have a lover?"

This time, I nearly choke. When Thane says 'lover' like that, I know he means 'mate', and the truth is that Rafe hasn't bonded with any demoness yet. However, that just means he hasn't found one to accept his essence while giving him hers. When it comes to the physical act of mating, of finding pleasure with any demoness that might accept his cock, that's not something that we talk about now that we're fully mature halflings with no sexual interest in each other.

"If he doesn't?" I sputter.

"Then he'll fetch a lot of gold from the slavers if they bring him to the Gilded Court. Even if the queen isn't interested, there are plenty of nobles who would be. Outsiders aren't welcome here," he murmurs softly, "but that doesn't mean that can't be used."

I don't even want to think about what Thane means by that. "I'll stop them. I'll save Rafe."

I have to.

"And I'll help you."

What? No. "You don't have to do that."

"There's quite a lot I don't have to do, Alana, but that's what makes me such a roguish bandit. Consider me your escort, no gold required."

"Until you sell me to the slavers and get all the gold they're willing to give you."

That would explain it—

"I can promise you that the slavers won't pay for a shadow-wielding demoness. Anything they want from you, they'll just take, and there isn't any soul in Noctavara who will stop them. Except me." Thane's gaze slides past me, into the dark between the trees. "Besides, if I wanted to sell you," he adds, "I wouldn't be standing here talking. I'd already have chains on your wrists."

My blood runs cold. "I appreciate your offer, but I think I'll go alone." My soul-pet nips my ear. "With Binx," I correct.

Thane gives my ungez an appraising look. He must be remembering the way that Binx attacked him, but all that does is tell him that, of the two of us, Binx is more dangerous than a Sombran halfling who can't use her shadows.

His next words confirm it: "The two of you can go alone. You'll just die together."

"We won't—"

He lifts a hand, palm up.

"You don't have to trust me, Alana of Sombra." He nods at my soul-pet. "Binx. You just have to trust this: you won't reach the Gilded Court without me. Not with horns. Not with shadows twisting around your feet." He jerks his chin up. "Not with a queen's butterfly nesting on your head."

I hate to admit that he has a point; more than a few, really. On more than one occasion, while Rafe and I were traveling in other realms, he had to come between a male and me who decided they wanted to claim me without wooing me first. Between his shadow barriers and my portals, we always escaped before anything could happen, but now I'm alone with Binx, and my shadows aren't working.

Even though I can't trust this fae, he *is* my mate. Whether he knows that now or not, a part of me instinctively *wants* to believe I should be able to trust him.

He's already proved he knows what he's talking about. There are obviously traps in the Shadowed

Woods. Bandits. If it's anything like the edge of shadows back home, there are monsters and beasts and I'll have to survive them all if I want to find Rafe —and that's nothing compared to what will happen if I do track down the slavers.

And then he says, "I'm only a danger to your gold, demoness. But seeing as you have none, I'm your best chance at going after your friend. Unless you'd rather return to Sombra for other reinforcements." He pauses. "Can you go back?"

I shake my head. "Even if I could, I wouldn't. Not without Rafe."

"Even if you have to go all the way to the Gilded Court to retrieve him?"

"There isn't anything I won't do to bring him home again."

Especially since I'm the reason he was left behind in Brille Rouge long enough for him to be taken…

Thane studies me for a long moment, and I'm starting to think he's decided to withdraw his offer of help when he lets out a soft breath.

"If you're set on going that far," he says, "there's something you should understand first. And I offer this for nothing but your agreement that you'll think about accepting my help."

"Why you?" I wonder. "Why does any of this mean that *you* need to help me?"

"Because a lone outsider doesn't reach the Gilded Court."

My fingers curl at my sides. "I can take care of myself."

"I don't doubt it," he replies easily. "In Sombra. In worlds where your shadows answer you. Not here."

I bristle. How does he know my shadows aren't working? I only said that I can't return to Sombra, nothing else... "You don't have any idea what I can do."

"No," he agrees. "But I know what *Noctavara* does to those who don't belong. And I know what the Court does when it sees something it wants."

Something—or someone.

"And what," I say carefully, "makes you think letting you join us will stop that from happening?"

In answer, he draws his sword. "This isn't just for saving pretty demonesses from snare traps."

Pretty demonesses... my cheeks heat, and I try to ignore it.

"And what do *you* get out of it?" I demand, fiercer than I mean to because, godsdamn it, he's getting under my skin.

His lips twitch. "You stay alive long enough to reach the queen's throne room."

"That's not an answer."

"It's the only one you need right now."

Of course. I guess I should be grateful I've gotten any at all.

"What if I decide you're a mistake?" I ask. "If I tell you to leave?"

Thane inclines his head. "Then I will."

And the fae can't lie…

I draw in a slow breath. "I don't have gold."

"I know."

"I won't owe you."

"You won't thank me," he corrects lightly. "That's enough."

Okay. Fine. "I'm considering it. So what did you want to tell me?"

He gestures vaguely at me. At my horns. At the shadows that still curl too close to my boots even thought I can't summon them the way I've always been able to. At the way Binx is nuzzled against my neck, the monarch butterfly still perched in my hair…

"All of that can be hidden with a simple fae glamour. But I can only hide so much, and nothing from the queen. And Queen Celeste doesn't allow shadow magic in Noctavara."

My spine tightens. That explains so much. Is that why I was blocked before? Why I haven't been able to open a portal to leave? Why my panties vanished, and Thane is better at disappearing into the darkness of the woods than I—one part shadow demon—is? If the ruler of this realm is against my type of immortal, what happens when the slavers bring Rafe in front of her?

And why is he telling me that *now*?

"Why doesn't she?" I ask.

His jaw works, like he's choosing how he wants to

word this. The fae can't lie, but that doesn't mean they always tell the truth—and that's something I must remember while I'm stuck in this world with someone who might have his own motivations to help me.

Finally, he answers me. "Because there's a prophecy."

That's the last thing I wanted to hear.

My stomach sinks. No. Absolutely not. It's bad enough that I overheard my parents talking about a second prophecy that involves me. I refuse to believe there could be a *third*.

"A prophecy?" I echo. "About what?"

"It doesn't concern a simple bandit. But I've heard things. There are stories," he continues. "Warnings. About outsiders who shouldn't exist in Noctavara, and how shadows cling to them even in the Shadowed Woods. The queen is very interested in their existence."

I know what he isn't saying. "She'll want Rafe."

"She might keep him. If you come for him, she might choose to keep you, too. And that's if she hasn't sensed your arrival in the Shadowed Woods already. The queen and the entire Gilded Court."

You know what? She can *try*.

I think of the butterfly in my hair. One of them brought me here. There has to be a way for it to guide me back to Sombra once I save Rafe. Maybe that's why my portals aren't working now. Deep down, I can't leave without him, and Binx agrees.

He bit Thane. If my soul-pet thought that the fae was a danger to me, he'd be flying at him, claws out, aiming for his eyes. He's not. Sure, Binx is watching Thane unblinkingly, but I can sense how my soul-pet trusts that my one true mate would want to help me, even if he doesn't *know* that he's mine just yet.

I'll have to tell him. If I agree to journey with Thane, I won't be able to keep that secret. For now, though, I have to think about how careful he's been to warn me against going after Rafe without insisting that I shouldn't.

It doesn't matter.

He's right. I need him, and not only because the gods have given me a tricky fae who seems too good to be true. He probably is, but I have to do everything I can for Rafe—including taking on a fae queen and her Court.

I lift my chin and meet his gaze head-on. The mate bond grows a little stronger as I see the honest if somewhat baffling offer of assistance in his amber eyes, and know that my own fear for Rafe and yearning for my one true mate reflect back in my golden ones.

I'm not afraid of this fae queen. I'm loyal to Apollyon and Lilith, the clan leader and clanmother. I obey—for the most part—Mom and Dad. My lieges are Duke Haures and Duchess Susanna of Sombra, not Queen Celeste of Noctavara and the Gilded Court.

They think they can stop me from saving Rafe?

"They might know. They might not. It doesn't matter. Tell them that I'm coming."

And when I get there—with Thane or not—I'll bring Rafe back to Sombra, then figure out what I'm supposed to do about having a fae mate.

CHAPTER 7
EAST

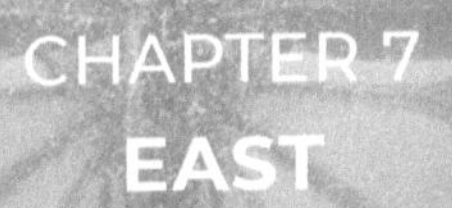

In the end, it's the mate bond that gets me to agree to stick around Thane.

I could say it's because he knows this world and I don't. I could pretend that I could get away from him if he proves to be *too* dangerous, that he's the best chance I have to find Rafe. He seems sure that it was slavers, not soldiers, that were searching Brille Rouge for demons they could sell to fae nobles in Noctavara. While we could try to find the caravans that house the slavers on their travels, it's better if we just assume that they're bringing Rafe to the Gilded Court—both the name for the nobles that serve her, plus the actual gilded structure where Queen Celeste has her seat of power.

And while all of that has a bit of truth to it, I'd be lying if I said that the fledgling bond that's taken root in my chest doesn't have the most to do with it. I didn't realize until after we were together again that it pulled, it tightened, it *stretched* as I left him. I'm just grateful that I don't have enough of my father's blood to go up in flames when I walk away from my future mate, though that could be because I'm closely guarding my essence.

Until he gives me his, I won't give him mine. That should save us from any other quirks—like the mate sickness or the fire—while I figure out if Thane can be my mate… and if I want him to.

Binx doesn't agree with me and my motives. It's clear that he would've rather we'd left Thane behind in the clearing. Since we didn't, my soul-pet stays perched high on my shoulder, fur bristling at the edges of his shadows, fluffy tail flicking in irritated swishes that keep brushing the side of my neck. If Thane so much as shifts too quickly, Binx's tiny claws dig into the fabric of my dress like he's preparing to launch himself at the fae again.

Thane, for his part, seems to find that amusing. I doubt he will if I stop holding Binx back with softly muttered warnings to behave, but it seems like the ungez is listening and the fae is safe from some scratches and bites.

There hasn't been another butterfly since I agreed to let Thane lead us in the direction he believes the slavers would've gone with Rafe. I'm not sure if that's a good sign or not. If we're heading the right way, maybe the monarch butterflies don't need to be a guide. Maybe they're wary of Thane, like I should be.

Or maybe I'm reading too much into an Earth butterfly that shouldn't be in this fae realm.

How did it get here? I know that Duke Haures is careful to keep the veil between Earth and Sombra closed, but with the right spell, it can open. I'm living proof that shadow walkers exist. I've been popping into Brille Rouge and Soleil since I was a young spawn. The slavers obviously have a way to travel from Noctavara and back. Could there be a way to travel from the fae realm to the human world?

If there is, I haven't been able to figure it out just yet. My shadows match our pace as we walk through the Shadowed Woods, but no matter how much I try to create a portal to go anywhere but here, it's like I'm blocked again.

I wasn't going to leave yet. Not without Rafe. Still, when I do find him, I'll need to find my way home again, and I only hope that I'll be able to.

For now, I focus on hoping that Rafe is okay, and that I'm not walking into a trap by following Thane so easily…

The fae bandit walks a few steps ahead of Binx and me, cloak dragging like darkness behind him, as he turns his head just enough to glance over his shoulder. He's been doing that every few minutes, as though making sure I haven't vanished on him, but this is the first time he speaks up.

"You're quiet," he tells me.

"I'm thinking," I reply automatically.

His lips quirk up in a sly grin. "Let me guess. You were thinking when you ran into a snare trap, too."

My jaw clenches. I open my mouth to snap something back at him, but before I can, something tugs low in my belly, like something's hooked inside of my navel and has been yanked.

The bond. That was our *bond*…

I shudder out a breath, deciding not to waste another with a snappish retort, telling him instead, "Never mind."

"If you say. But, you know, you don't have to bristle every time I speak. I'm only teasing."

If that's what he wants to call it. "I don't bristle."

"You do," he says simply, and that—his calm certainty that he's right—makes me want to bristle harder.

The dark forest floor is soft beneath my boots, damp and springy, nothing like ash. It gives without crumbling, and that should be comforting, but it isn't. It's too alive. The trees here don't just exist. They *loom*. The silver moon overhead helps me see where I'm going, but the way it enhances the soft glow of Thane's golden skin is even more distracting.

Add that to the grin tugging on his lips, and I have to work to hide my scowl.

So I force my gaze away from his shoulders, from the elegant tilt of his pointed ear beneath the hood of his cloak, from the way the fabric of that cloak sways around his legs like he's the one who's made of shadows... I force my attention away from Thane, looking down at the path instead.

The path—or what passes for one.

Thane doesn't follow trails the way a demon would; except, perhaps, for a Sombran hunter like Dagon or Nox. He doesn't pick the clearest route or the straightest line. He moves like he's seeing something I can't, like the forest is a map only he can read. Sometimes he veers left without warning. Sometimes he pauses and listens, head cocked, amber eyes narrowing at nothing.

Every time he does, my body reacts. I feel heat pooling down in the lower part of my belly, watching him closely as though I can't resist the pull. It's the mate bond again, I know it is, and considering this is the worst possible moment for me to feel so very drawn to a stranger, I hate it.

I also... *don't.*

Crud.

HOURS INTO OUR WALK—AND NOT THAT MUCH longer after I realized they were missing— a trio of monarch butterflies appear, fluttering in and out of view like I can't be sure if they're real or if I'm seeing things.

Sometimes they dart ahead, bright against the dark. Sometimes they vanish completely.

Sometimes one lingers near my hair, close enough that I can feel the brush of air from its wings against my pointed ear, my cheek.

Thane notices every time with a narrowing of his gaze.

He doesn't comment on the butterflies again—not directly—but I catch him glancing at them with a tightness around his mouth that wasn't there before when he was enjoying himself teasing me.

"What?" I ask finally, after the third time he looks like he's swallowed something pointy.

His eyes slide over to me. "I can't tell if you're following them or if the queen's butterflies are chasing after you."

My shadows curl around my boots, more transparent than they usually are. They don't gather. They don't *listen*. They just… exist, thin and frustrated, like a limb I can't fully use.

I glance down at them and grit my teeth.

"Can you stop saying 'queen' like that?" I mutter. "It makes it sound like these are her pets, the way Binx is mine. Like she's… everywhere."

Thane's mouth curves faintly. It's not quite a smile, though I can't miss the slightly mocking edge to it. "Who says that she isn't?"

Oh, I don't like the way he said that. I don't like that at all.

Sensing my sudden unease, Binx shifts on my shoulder, pressing his small body against my throat. His white eyes glow brighter in the dark.

Protective.

I stroke his shadow-fur with my fingertips until he settles, but I don't take my gaze off Thane.

"If Queen Celeste doesn't allow shadow magic," I ask carefully, "then why do I still have any of mine at all?"

Weak they might be, but my shadows are still here. That gives me hope that I can use them again—until the fae dashes them.

Thane slows just enough that his cloak stops swaying. He turns more fully, walking backward for a few steps while he studies me as though really seeing me for the first time.

"You're not fae," he says once more, gaze settling on my horns again, a sure marker that I'm at least part demon. "You're not bound to her laws in the same way the rest of us are."

"So I can use my shadows."

His gaze drops to the thin curl of darkness at my feet. "In theory."

My jaw tightens. "In reality, she won't let me."

Thane's eyes narrow. "You feel it."

Yeah. In ways I can't quite describe to someone who isn't made up of shadows like I am, yeah. I feel it. "I'm not stupid," I tell him.

He huffs a laugh, quick and quiet. "No. You're brave, Alana of Sombra."

Maybe, but I'm definitely in trouble again. Whether or not she has any idea what happened to a demon stolen by slavers from her realm, something tells me that—if I want to leave Noctavara after following the monarch butterfly into her realm—I'll have to face Queen Celeste eventually. Is that why the butterflies are here? The queen's butterflies… are they making sure I reach the monarch of this realm?

I don't know, though my instincts tell me that I *do*. I open my mouth to ask Thane how much of a death wish it is for an immortal halfling to request an audience with the queen of this realm when Thane stops walking backward and turns again, slipping seamlessly ahead of me as if the conversation is done.

Not for me it isn't. And while I hold off on asking him about the queen, I have another question on my mind.

"Where exactly are we going?" I demand, louder than I mean to. Luckily, the woods swallow the sound so that only the three of us hear it.

Thane doesn't look back. "East."

I glance around. "Sorry, but that means nothing to me."

"It will." He dares a peek over his shoulder at me. Then, as though he's taken pity on the outsider, he says, "East will lead us to the edge of the Shadowed Woods. There's a road beyond it, out of reach of the other bandits and beasts in the woods. You'll find traders. Inns. Maybe even the slavers who have your demon. If not, we'll take the road until it ends."

"At the Gilded Court?"

"At the Court," he agrees.

It's a plan. That's what I needed. I'm not just walking around aimlessly, hoping I'll stumble on Rafe. I have a purpose, and no matter what, I'll do it.

Rafe…

I keep seeing him in my mind's eye: his pale hair, his purple eyes, that grin of his when he's being his charming and ridiculous self, and the earnestness he can't hide when he's trying so hard to be taken seriously as a male and not a halfling spawn.

And then, because I can't stop myself, I see him creating the protective barrier made of his shadows, shielding Katrin and the other demonesses, before being put in chains and dragged by soldiers… slavers… *fae* who captured him all because I left him alone in Brille Rouge for too long…

Guilt is a bitter thing. It sits in my throat and makes everything else taste wrong. Binx chuffs, letting me know he's right there with me. With a small, shaky smile, I swallow roughly and keep on moving.

Thane walks without any obvious effort, but neither is he rushing. He keeps a pace I can follow, and that—as tiny as it is—does something to my chest. He could lose me easily, changing his mind about helping me, but he doesn't—and I don't know what to think about that other than maybe he senses the fledgling bond between us, too.

And every time I think that, he opens his mouth and says something that reminds me that he's just the cocky guide I didn't ask for.

"Keep moving," he says as I slow a little, gaze on his back because, well, I can't stop myself. "And stay right behind me when we cross streams."

There's been at least a demon's length between us as we walked. I figured he was avoiding the butterflies, but now I'm not so sure. "Why?"

"Because the banks are soft."

Okay. "And?"

"And I don't want to yank you out of the mud," he says. "Again."

I glower. "Once," I tell him. "That happened once." And I have dark mud all over my boots as a reminder to be careful where I'm walking in this strange world.

Thane's mouth twitches, though he doesn't say anything else. Still, it's the closest thing to a smile he's given me since he told me where we were headed, and I can't deny that the bond deep in my chest almost *pulses*.

Binx nips my ear hard enough to make me hiss, forgetting the mate bond for a moment.

"Fine," I mutter, rubbing my ear even though I'm grateful that, through my bond with my soul-pet, Binx gave me just the sort of distraction I could use. Rafe, I tell myself. Focus on Rafe, not the fae. "Fine. I'm moving."

And if I can't resist the urge to shove Thane in the mud next time, well… they can't be helped, can it?

He gets lucky. For the rest of the eve, I'm on my best behavior because I start to get tired; while full-blooded demons need only a few hours of rest a night, halflings take after our human parents in that regard. I'm desperate to take a break, though I don't tell him so. Instead, staying close to Thane, we keep on walking until the light shining down on us shifts.

It's subtle at first. The moon is still overhead, silver and bright, but the shadows beneath the trees deepen. The air cools, though it's more of a breeze against my overheated skin. It grows heavier, though, and it isn't long before Thane slows.

I stop automatically, even though he doesn't tell me to. I'll take any excuse for a small break.

While I bend low, flicking some of the dried mud off of my right boot, he listens.

That catches my attention. As he shifts slightly, cocking his head, everything in me goes tight. Binx goes still on my shoulder, ears pricked, body taut. And the butterflies… they're gone.

I wait.

Then, faintly, there's a sound. A rustle, low and distant, but audible. I think… I think something's moving through the trees. Something big enough to shift branches, but careful enough that it doesn't snap them.

My heart jumps, then pounds. I reach for Binx, who nuzzles against my trembling fingers.

Thane doesn't draw his sword. Not yet. He just angles his head, gaze fixed into the dark between the tree trunks.

After a long moment, the sound fades. Thane exhales, slow and quiet.

Turning to me, he asks, "You hear that?"

"Yes," I admit.

"Good," he says before turning away. "That means you'll hear it next time sooner."

I gulp. "Next time?" Scurrying forward, clutching his arm while purposely blocking any essence exchange between us, I repeat, "Next time?"

His mouth curves again. "And that's if the Shadowed Woods gives you any warning."

Oh, I don't like that. I don't like that *at all*.

My throat starts to ache long before I'm willing to admit it.

At first, I try to ignore it. I've gone longer without water in Sombra, but that's only because there's a running tap in every home to quench our thirst and fill our baths. I have a fondness for javitz—or coffee in Human—which is also made with water. Whenever I'm thirsty, I can have a drink… only not in Noctavara.

We pass streams. Thane off-handedly tells Binx that he'll toss him in the next one if he thinks of biting him again, but just when I think I should give him a shove into the muddy stream, he offers me his hand to help me cross it.

He does not, however, give me the chance to stop and see if the water is drinkable.

Once I start thinking about how thirsty I am, I

remember that I never had anything past the midday meal, either. The thirst is a bigger concern, but I'm going to need to eat soon, too. I don't even realize how much it's affecting me until my steps have slowed just enough for Thane to notice.

"You're dragging," he points out.

"I'm not," I reply, the lie scraping my dry throat on the way out. Crud. My words are raspy, my throat pinchy enough that I wince.

His amber eyes flick down to my mouth, then back up again.

Without a word, Thane shoves back his cloak. Earlier, I noticed the sheath that holds his blade, but nothing else. As his hand goes to his waist, I see that he has at least three bundles or satchels attached at his hip. There's something else, I notice, and I realize what it is when he pulls free a dark leather canteen, worn smooth from use.

He uncorks it, offering it to me. "You look like you need a sip."

I hesitate.

Every story I've ever read about fae realms flickers through my mind at once. I don't know whether they're true or not, but apart from learning that the fae can't tell a lie, I remember the warning that you should never eat or drink anything that comes from Faerie.

Faerie is the main realm for the fae. Other worlds, like Arcadia or Noctavara, branch off from it; they're usually neighboring worlds, like how Brille Rouge and Soleil are so close to Sombra, even with a few differences between the types of demons. I don't know how many of their rules transfer here, but if I accept his canteen—if I take that sip—and I end up being bound to this world?

No, thanks.

I only hope that's not the case. I'm not so thirsty that I'm willing to wager my freedom, but it's only been a couple of hours. What if it takes a lot longer? Days? Moons?

I dart out my tongue, dabbing the corner of my mouth. "Depends. What is it?"

His eyes flicker in amusement. "If I had faerie wine, I wouldn't be sharing it, if that's what you mean. It's water, demoness. Fresh spring water that I gathered this morning instead of risking a bellyache from the shadowed streams in the woods."

"And it's safe?"

A corner of his mouth lifts. "As safe as anything in Noctavara can be. Go on. Take what you need. I can always refill it later."

He has a point. So, snorting despite myself, I take the canteen, careful not to let my fingers brush his any more than necessary.

The water is cool and clean, just like the water from home. I take one swallow, then another, greedier this time, until the ache in my throat eases and my shoulders finally loosen.

When I hand it back, he corks it again, then tucks it away.

I don't feel any different; other than my thirst being quenched, that is. If I can trust the water, then maybe… I think of the bundles on his waist. "Do you have anything to eat? That's safe for someone like me?"

"You're right to be cautious," he says. "Eating in Noctavara can be… tricky. Just don't eat any faerie fruit, or accept anything from Queen Celeste, and you should be fine." Again, his slender fingers go to his waist. He grabs one of the bundles, giving it a jingle. Something metal clanks together. "That would be my gold." The next one makes no sound. "Ah. Here we go."

Thane removes it from his belt, tossing it to me. The leatherskin pouch has a drawstring. I open it, Binx climbing down my arm so that he can stick his twitching nose inside.

"I borrowed it from a bandit cache. In case I can't go hunting or haven't bought fresh food from one of the traders on the main road, I always make sure I have something ready to eat. Dried meat. Cured cheeses. Salted roots. Things that don't spoil. Have some. Binx, too."

I already hear crunching as Binx finds something in the pouch that interests him.

Me? I'm more curious about what Thane just said. "What exactly is a bandit cache?"

Thane shakes his shoulders, letting his cloak fall back in place. "I told you, Alana. There are plenty of creatures that haunt these woods. Some of them are like me. Bandits. We have a code. We help each other when we can. That's the caches. If you have extra meat you can't carry, leave it behind. If you need a new cloak, someone might have one for you. It's how we all survive the woods."

I want to ask him why they'd even want to. Trudging through the dark woods, avoiding any unseen beasts that might think that *we're* a snack... there has to be more to Noctavara than that.

However, before I can ask—or because he can sense I'm about to—Thane pulls his hood up, covering his dark curls, his handsome face, the knowing look in his amber eyes.

"Eat up," he says shortly. "We should probably find another cache to restock before the moon goes down."

And, fledgling bond or not, I know instinctively that the matter is closed.

For now.

ABOUT AN HOUR OR SO LATER, WE STOP NEAR A cluster of roots that rise out of the ground like knuckles, thick and gnarled. The air here is colder. The bark of the trees is paler, almost luminous in the moonlight.

Thane lifts a hand, signaling me to stop.

I do, immediately. My sudden pause rouses Binx. The ungez was snuffling softly, wrapped around my neck, lulled to sleep during the last leg of our trek. Lifting his head, he makes a questioning sound.

I kind of want to do the same.

Thane scans the area once, then twice. Only when he seems satisfied does he step toward one of the trees, trailing his fingers over the trunk.

"This is far enough for tonight," he announces.

Already?

"We're stopping?" I ask. "Why? We've only been walking for—"

"Long enough," he cuts in. "You're not used to Noctavara." He gestures over his head at what I assumed was the moon until he says, "The sun will be setting soon. Dark will follow. It won't be safe to continue walking and, besides, you're tired."

"I'm not—"

"You are," he says, "and so am I."

I'm more surprised that he admitted it than that he's grown tired at all. Still…

"I need to keep going," I insist, softer this time. "Rafe—"

"If you push until you collapse, you won't survive long enough to find him. Immortal or not."

The bluntness of his words hits like a slap, especially after Mom put 'dying' and 'Noctavara' in my head at the same time earlier today.

After a moment, I swallow the snappish retort I wanted to let out and, instead, I nod.

"Fine," I manage. "We stop."

Thane gives a small nod in return, like we just negotiated a treaty instead of the fact that we're probably both too exhausted to argue anymore.

He steps away from the tree and gestures toward a patch of ground where the strange grass looks thicker. Softer.

I hesitate.

"Do you want me to lay out a blanket, too, demoness?" he asks with a hint of a smirk.

I glare over at him. "I don't know what you have," I say, allowing myself to snap this time. "And I didn't realize you meant we had to sleep outside."

"What you see is what you get," he says, gesturing at his belt. "I can gather more supplies in the morning, but this is everything." He pauses. "Bandit, remember?"

"Yeah, I remember," I mutter, shaking my head. "It's fine. We'll be fine. Right, Binx?"

Binx makes a soft sound of agreement, more for my sake than Thane's.

I lower us carefully, skirts gathered in my hands so I don't snag them on the roots. The ground is damp, but not so cold that it cuts through the woven fabric made for me from the best seamstresses in Nuit. Still,

I can't relax fully. My shadows curl closer to my boots, like they're trying to shield me, while Binx hops down from my shoulder and circles once, twice, before curling up on my lap with his tail wrapped around his body. His white eyes remain open, watching the dark.

Thane stands a few paces away, scanning the trees again, and I realize he hasn't sat. He hasn't even shifted his weight like he's preparing to join us on the ground.

"Aren't you gonna get some rest?" I ask before I can stop myself.

Thane glances at me. "You need to."

"Yeah, but what about you?"

He pauses, then gestures upward.

It takes me a moment to see what he means. The branches above us are thick. High. Some of them stretch out like platforms, broad enough that someone could lie across them if they were…

If they were fae.

If they were used to this world.

"You're sleeping up there?"

"Yes."

"Why?"

"So I can watch for danger," he replies, like it's obvious.

I scoff. "So you can run if you see something coming."

His eyes narrow. "So I can kill it before it gets to you."

Oh.

My stomach goes tight, the bond strengthening just a little more at his honesty. He means it. If some kind of threat finds us in the shadows, he'll protect me. He only just met me, but for reasons I can't understand—and only hope are the same as mine—this fae is willing to keep me safe.

And that's not all.

As I keep an eye on him, Thane shrugs out of his cloak. Before I can even guess what he's about to do, he drops it in my lap, earning a squeak from Binx as it covers the ungez.

Thane's lips twitch before he swallows his grin. "Here. This should keep you warm."

"Won't you be cold?"

"Nah. I really only wear it so that I can skulk around the woods without anyone seeing me. I'll take the high ground tonight. It's better that you have the cloak 'til morning."

I don't argue with him. Lifting the blanket off of Binx, I run my fingers over the heavy fabric. "You know, they told me that Noctavara was home to fire demons."

"We're fae. A sect of the Seelie with an affinity for gold. But since we're not supposed to leave, those who do—"

"Like the slavers?"

He nods. "They don't bother concealing their golden skin with cloaks. All it takes is a little glamour to give them horns when they're… hunting. And there you go. Fire demons. Here in Noctavara, we can be who we want to be."

"Like a bandit?" I ask, spreading the cloak out on my lap. It holds Thane's heat, carrying his scent with him. Something addictive and musky and pure *him.*

Godsdamn it, but it smells amazing.

"That's right, demoness," he says before jerking his chin at me. "Comfortable?"

I ignore the return of the slight tease to his voice. "Yes." I pause, my instincts suddenly screaming to say 'thank you', because my mother and father raised me with manners even if there are those in Nuit who would disagree.

Thane's expression tightens, almost like he can see the words forming on my tongue.

"Don't," he warns.

I snap my mouth shut.

Binx makes a sound that might be an ungez laugh. Considering I can sense his amusement skittering down our soulbond, I know that that's exactly what it is. Looks like he's forgiven Thane for dropping the cloak on top of him, the fuzzy traitor.

Thane gives me a satisfied look before he moves.

One moment he was standing in front of me. The next, he's stepping onto the roots, gripping the bark with hands that shouldn't be able to cling to the smooth silver wood that make up the tree's trunk, and then he's up, disappearing into the branches like he belongs there.

I stare upward, oddly nervous for reasons I don't want to look too closely at.

Thane settles on a thick branch above me, not directly overhead but close enough that if he moves, I'll hear the shifting of the leaves. His silhouette blends into the darkness except for the faint gold glow of his skin, but it seems to dim compared to how strong it was hours ago. Almost as though the shadows of the Shadowed Woods are swallowing him whole.

Amber eyes watch me from above.

"Sleep," he calls down to me, tone shifting again, the command softer now. "Your friend needs you rested and alive."

Rafe.

Where is he now? Is he safe? Have the slavers fed him or have they bound him? Will I be able to take him from this realm when I find him? Am I fooling myself that I actually will? I thought it would be as easy as walking into Noctavara, grabbing Rafe, and going home. Nope. Now I'm leaning back against a tree with a fae bandit in it, my parents have no idea where I am—though, considering it's Noctavara, that's probably a good thing for Mom's nerves—and I've never felt less immortal in my existence.

But Thane is right. I need sleep.

I close my eyes. My shadows nestle beneath me,

Binx already snuffling his snores as he snuggles against Thane's cloak. I try, but I don't fall asleep immediately. Whether it's because I can sense Thane's presence over my head or because my instincts are telling me to go to him, to curl up next to him, to tell him he's my mate… without the walking to distract me, all I can think of is what's going on with Rafe and Thane, and I don't know which one is worse.

Eventually, exhaustion and worry win, and I can only hope I'm not making a fatal mistake, trusting Thane Aurex.

I wake up the next morning warmer than I thought I'd be.

Not because the forest has brightened. It hasn't. The Shadowed Woods remain steeped in its eternal twilight, like Earth does after its vibrant sun sets, but I *feel* the shift.

So it's morning, then, or whatever passes for it here.

I'm lying on my side, wrapped up in Thane's cloak, my hair a knotted mess beneath my head. Sitting up slowly, I brush one of the tangled snarls away from my left horn. The movement rouses Binx. He yawns widely, showing off his adorable fangs.

I ruffle his shadowy fur, glancing around for Thane. I expected to find him up in the trees so I'm slightly surprised to notice him standing about three demon's lengths away, fiddling with the pouches on his belt.

Once I've used my claws to smooth out my hair, I gather the cloak around my body and rise, padding closer to him. "You should have woken me."

He glances over his shoulder, giving no sign of any surprise of his own that I'm up. "You needed the rest."

I remove the cloak, holding it out to him. *Don't say thank you, don't say thank you…* "This is yours."

He hesitates, as though he hears the words I really want to say. Then he takes the cloak from my hands, flips it over his shoulders, and slings it back on. Once he has, he grabs something near his feet.

It's the canteen.

"And this one's yours," Thane tells me.

I blink. Glancing down at his waist, I see the one he let me drink out of yesterday. "Mine?"

He nods once and presses it into my hands. It's newer than the one he offered me last night, the leather unbroken, the seal super tight when start to turn the lid.

"You'll need it," he adds. "We're moving out soon."

I cracked the seal, but I don't take a swig just yet. "I don't have anything to trade you for it."

His mouth quirks, just barely. "Not yet you don't."

I give Thane a curious look.

"When you find gold of your own, you can give

me a coin and we'll call it even." A whisper of a taunting smile tugs on his lips as I put the open canteen to mine. "Believe me, Alana, you don't want to be in debt to anyone in Noctavara."

Oh, trust me, Thane. I *know*.

I DON'T KNOW HOW LONG WE'VE BEEN WALKING WHEN it happens.

The funny thing—or, really, *not* so funny thing—is that I feel it before I hear it. The woods around us have gone quiet; not peaceful, but more alert. Like everything lurking inside of it has just decided to hold its breath and wait and see what's going to happen next.

Binx stiffens against my calf, radiating concern. *Danger.* That's the emotion singing down the bond between me and my soul-pet. He senses danger.

I open my mouth to warn Thane, but he's already moving.

"Stay behind me," he says, voice light. Too light for the way his hand drops to the hilt of his sword in between steps.

Right as he draws it, something lunges from the shadows.

It's fast. *Too* fast. A blur of teeth and something dark and hungry aimed right at my throat.

All I see is wood-colored skin, rags that match the

shadows, and a dark gold, crusty hat covering its gnarled head. The creature itself would come up to my navel if it were standing. It must have some powerful legs because its flight carries it toward my head, fangs bared as though it plans on ripping out my throat before devouring the rest of me.

Thane moves, dancing between it and me.

His sword whistles as the steel flashes. The sound it makes when his blade connects with the beast isn't a clean slice. Nope. It's wet. *Final.* Immortal or not, the creature hits the ground in two distinct pieces, the gold cap falling off of its separated head before the body itself dissolves into black smoke that joins the shadows.

I barely have time to register that when another comes from the left.

Then another.

Thane doesn't hesitate. He pivots, precise and brutal, sword moving like it's an extension of his arm. There's no wasted motion as he slaughters the fae beasts. Each one disintegrates once it's dead, and I lose count after the third one.

That was my mistake. Watching Thane, I stopped looking for more threats. One of the fierce monsters manages a swipe that cuts through the long sleeve of my dress before Thane swings his sword again. Unfortunately, that gives another one the chance to swipe at Thane, finding the underside of his sword arm before he dispatches it.

Finally, it just… *stops*. Thane steps back, chest heaving notably, dark curls falling forward into his amber eyes. He doesn't look winded the way a mortal would. He looks… *alive*. Like the violence woke something up inside of him, and now it's purring in a way that reminds me of Binx.

Binx, meanwhile, makes a low, offended sound at my feet. The ungez's fluffy shadow-tail lashes once, twice, and his white eyes narrow at the gold-colored hat that's all that's left on the creatures.

"You can stop glaring at it," I murmur. "They're all gone."

He chitters, indignation humming through the bond that the beast dared to try attack me. At the same time, I sense his approval that Thane was quick enough to end them before they could pull it off.

I assure Binx that I'm okay—and then realize I'm lying to myself when the delayed sting catches up with me and, in response to the pain, I hiss through my teeth.

Thane's gaze snaps to me. Lowering his sword down at his side, he stalks over to me.

"Show me," he demands.

That's not a request. It's not a suggestion, either. It's the kind of tone I've heard from Mom when I try to hide something from her… the kind that I know better than to ignore.

I shove my sleeve up and lift my arm reluctantly.

A thin line of blood beads along the top of my

arm where something clawed me. It's nothing deep, but it's undeniable that one of the beasts got me. As we look, my black blood is already slicking down toward my wrist.

In the dim twilight, it looks like shining ink.

Thane goes very still.

He doesn't flinch like my mother did the first time she saw it. Mom screamed then—full, human panic—because she'd spent a lifetime believing blood was supposed to be red, and because the sight of mine was another reminder that I was as much my father's daughter as hers. Though that didn't really help, either, since Sombra demons don't bleed black.

Only halflings do, as though that's a hint of the shadows we can't quite control like our demon parent.

"Interesting," he says at last in a voice too careful to do anything other than get my heart racing.

I swallow, forcing myself calm. "What? It's just blood."

"It's not the color I'm used to." His gaze drags up from the cut to my face. "How bad does it hurt?"

"I've had worse."

His jaw tightens like he doesn't like that answer, but that doesn't stop him from reaching for me.

That doesn't, but my ungez might. Before Thane can touch me, Binx hisses, an ugly little sound that doesn't belong to something that looks as cute as he is. His claws catch at my collar as if he's preparing to launch himself.

Thane freezes mid-motion.

For a heartbeat, we all hold still: me, him, and my protective soul-pet.

Then Thane's mouth curves.

"Ah," he says, eyes flicking to Binx with open fascination. "So *that's* what you are."

Binx chitters at me, letting me know that he doesn't like the way the fae is staring at him.

"He's never seen an ungez," I tell Binx under my breath. "And you hissed at him after he saved us."

I don't say thank you. I can't. But despite the gratitude underlying my rebuke, he pays closer attention to Binx.

Thane's brows lift. "Ungez?"

"It's what Binx is. In Sombra, it means he bites first and asks questions never," I say, and my tease comes out drier than I mean it to.

Binx makes a pleased, smug little noise at my description of him.

Thane nods. "It's good. He's obviously loyal to you."

"Because he's bonded to me," I explain. That's what it is. Binx isn't a pet the way humans mean it. He's a piece of my soul given claws and attitude and all because he picked me when I was a spawn. "And it doesn't hurt. Not really. Demons heal quickly." Quicker still if I could tap into my shadows. "I'll be fine."

"If you say so."

I do. Tugging down my sleeve, hiding the cut, I use the toe of my boot to gesture at the cap left behind. "What were those things?"

Thane's gaze shifts to it, and something in his face hardens. "Hunters."

"Hunters of what?" I ask.

His eyes slide back to me. "Outsiders."

I gulp. "Oh."

There's a slight flash in the depth of his amber gaze. "They're called goldcaps. If they have another name for the ferocious critters, I don't know it. They attack travelers, aiming to kill that which shouldn't be killed. And when they do?" Thane crouches down, using the point of his sword to lift up the crusted-over hat that the goldcap was wearing. "They dip their caps into the blood of their victims. That's why they're called goldcaps."

I frown. "Who bleeds gold like that here?"

A quick flick of his wrist sends the cap back to the ground. After resheathing his sword, Thane shrugs his cloak back so that he can show me the long scratch down the underside of his forearm. "The fae of Noctavara do."

The glimmering, golden line doesn't look *real*. It looks like pure Earth sunlight distilled into a liquid smeared on his equally gold skin, seeping from a shallow cut on his arm where one of the creatures got him before he killed it.

"You're hurt," I gasp.

"It's nothing." He moves like he means to turn away.

Surging forward, I catch his wrist.

It's stupid.

It's reckless.

It's—

His gaze snaps to where my fingers wrap around him.

Heat floods up my arm. Not from his skin—though he's warm, absurdly warm—but from the jolt of contact, the way the bond in my chest reacts like a living thing. I hold onto my essence so I don't accidentally share it with Thane. Throwing up a block, I refuse to take anything from my mate that he's not aware he might be giving me.

But, still, I maintain the contact between us, stunned when Thane doesn't pull away.

He looks down at my hand on his wrist, then up at my face. The brightness in his eyes darkens into something almost hungry.

For one fragile heartbeat, I forget about Rafe, then I hate myself that I did. Nothing can happen until I find him, but if the goldcaps attack again, I finally admit to myself that I *do* need Thane's help. It's not only because the bond is tugging me toward him… oh, no. I need his sword and his supplies, and to make sure he isn't hurt—

"You're bleeding," I point out stupidly.

Thane glances at his arm like he's surprised to

find the cut still there. "More gold," he murmurs. "Does it offend you?"

"It… glows," I say as I hurriedly release him. That's the problem right there. It's too beautiful to be blood.

Just like Thane's too beautiful for a halfling who's in way over her horns.

His mouth twitches, visibly amused, which is something considering he's bleeding more than I was. "It's not meant to be admired."

"I'm not admiring it," I lie.

Binx chitters, pointedly saying something like: *You are.*

Thane's gaze flicks to Binx again, suddenly amused. "Let me guess. He's calling you a fibber, demoness."

"He's honest with me," I correct.

Thane's smile turns faintly wicked. "That must be convenient."

I narrow my eyes. "Are you mocking me?"

"No," he says, too quick and too smooth. "Just trying to figure out what it means to have a bond with another creature."

Oof. The way he says that… "And you don't have any?"

He opens his mouth, but I realize that I don't want to hear his answer.

"Forget it." I take a slow breath to steady myself.

"We should get out of here before anything else wants to attack."

Thane doesn't move. Not yet. Instead, he leans down, scoops a handful of dark dirt, and presses it against his cut without flinching. The gold smears and dulls beneath the grime.

"I don't want anything tracking us," he explains.

Uh-oh… "Something tracks blood?"

"In these woods?" He straightens. "Everything."

Binx makes a small, disgusted noise, pressing closer to my neck. I adjust my sleeve, glad that the blood's not seeping through the black fabric, then glance at Thane's arm again.

From what I can see, his cut is already slowing. The blood is still gold, but there's less of it now.

Right. Because he's fae. He's immortal.

He can be mine for eternity…

"Demons heal fast," I blurt out since I don't know what else to do with the question that's building behind my fangs. "I guess fae can, too."

Thane tilts his head. "What kind of demoness are you, Alana? You've said your from a plane called Sombra, but you seem… more than that."

From the moment he saw my horns, he knew I was a demoness; he's even called me that instead of my given name. But the way he asks that now… he suspects that I'm not quite what I appear.

He's right. What kind of demoness am I? The

answer is complicated unless you know Sombra's history.

"I'm a halfling," I admit at last. "Half-human. Half-Sombra demon."

He studies me as if he can see the split down to my bones. "And which half bleeds black?"

"Neither," I mutter.

A laugh escapes him. It's soft and genuine, but gone too quickly. "And your friend?" he asks, nodding to Binx.

"My soul-pet," I correct automatically.

Thane's brows rise. "Soul?" For a moment, his gaze lingers on Binx's glowing eyes. Then his attention goes back to me, and his voice is careful again. "That's right. You were just saying how demons form bonds. With… ungez, was it?"

Crud.

That's not a question. That's a *trap*.

I force myself to keep my face neutral. "It's not just the ungez. We also have mates." I pause for a moment, remembering the word he used yesterday. "Lovers. They take part of our soul, then give us part of theirs, and it's a bonded matrimony that can never be broken."

Unless you appeal to Duke Haures, gather the ashbalm flower, and break the mate bond… but who would do that?

Thane stays quiet.

I can't.

"Do fae?" I ask as casually as I can manage.

Binx's tail flicks once against my collarbone, a warning to be careful. I know, bud. I know.

Thane's mouth tightens, his gaze turning away from me. "No."

"Not ever?" I press before I can stop myself.

His eyes cut back to mine. "Not here."

The emphasis means something. I just wish I knew *what.*

"Why not?" I ask.

He exhales through his nose. It almost sounds like a laugh, but there's no humor in it. Not this time.

"Because Noctavara doesn't allow it," he says.

Something in my chest goes tight.

Not *can't.*

Not *doesn't happen.*

Not *we don't want them.*

Noctavara doesn't *allow* them.

Oh, no, no, no…

"And if someone…" I begin.

Thane's gaze flicks to my mouth. To my throat. To the place on my skin where he held his blade when we first met.

"Don't," he says softly.

Again with the don'ts.

I swallow. "Must be lonely."

His mouth curves faintly. "It's all I've ever known, demoness."

Then, with an effort that feels practiced, he

straightens and rolls his shoulders like he can shake off the weight of that admission.

"Come," he says, voice returning to the same pleasant tone he uses when he's not being cocky or demanding. "With all the blood spilled here, it's a wonder we haven't attracted any other creatures. We should be going if you don't want your friend to get too far ahead."

So, according to Thane, the fae don't have bonds. Then explain how he's been able to figure me out so soon already? Using Rafe against me…

I make sure Binx is settled, then nod. "Lead the way, bandit."

CHAPTER 10

MORGANE

I was beginning to think that Thane was the only bandit in this part of the Shadowed Woods. Sure, he keeps leading us to the bandit caches he mentioned—small hideaways tucked beneath the strange grass that he calls moss or in the dark holes of the silver-barked trees—so that he can replenish our supplies, but even after the goldcaps tried to kill us, I don't expect to run into another fae male lurking through the woods.

That was another mess-up on my part. Like most things in my life, I blame it on being the chosen one back when I was an infant. Somehow, I convinced myself that I'll always be safe, always be protected, and even if I'm not, there isn't anything I can't do.

That's why I refused to return to Sombra for help. It's my fault that Rafe was left behind in Brille Rouge to be taken, and I'm going to prove that the gods saw something in me that I've never been able to by rescuing him on my own. Binx could help me, and I don't think I can shake Thane at this point if I wanted to, but I honestly believed I wasn't in any danger.

Yeah, well, tell that to the bloodstain on my sleeve.

Still, more confident than I have any right to be, I moved on from the goldcap attack believing that was the worst the Shadowed Woods could throw at us. If anything, I'm worried about walking into the Gilded Court, possibly coming face-to-face with Queen Celeste, and appealing to the fae queen for aid in retrieving Rafe from a member of her Court. Danger in the woods? With Thane taking the lead, I wasn't worried about anything happening to me.

At least, not until I understand exactly *why* he insisted on joining me on my search.

Part of me wants to believe it's our mate bond at work. Maybe he doesn't think I understand what it means to experience a fated mate bond; since I've done everything I can to ignore it so far, he might not even know that I'm aware who he is. Of course, that's assuming *he* knows...

Either way, I'm stuck with him, and I guess it could've been worse. If I have to rely on a bandit, if I have to trust him around Binx and believe he'll help me find Rafe, then I'll do my best to do so. At least *I* know he's meant to be mine and, just because of that, I feel a sense of trust building thanks to the whisper-thin bond stretching between us.

Okay, and maybe I put a little too much faith into an armed stranger I barely met. I don't really have a choice. Until my shadows decide to listen to me and allow me to create a portal so I can escape Noctavara if I have to, me and Binx are stuck with Thane.

Which isn't really that bad when we finally do run into another bandit...

The fae male doesn't announce his presence so much as he *decides* to let himself be seen.

That's the only way I can describe it. One moment, the woods are still like they have been. The next, he's there. His cloak shadowing him, a soft glow peeking through the seam before he throws back the hood, I have to do a double-take when I see him.

His features are similar to Thane's at first glance. The same amber eyes, the same glowing skin, the same lithe and limber build. He also has a sword on his belt and a daring gleam in his eye, but despite being as beautiful as Thane, I notice enough small differences to know that while he's a Noctavaran fae, he's not *my* fae.

He's a touch taller, giving the impression that he's been stretched out. His hair—as black as Thane's—is thick and straight, pulled away from his face. His nose is a little longer. And, well, he's not my mate which means that I'm nitpicking, but he's nowhere near as captivating as Thane is.

"Well, well," a voice drawls pleasantly, his fae

accent obvious, "this stretch of the Shadowed Woods grows more interesting by the decade."

Thane doesn't turn his attention to the other male right away.

I do.

As I stare at him, the fae bandit steps fully into view, golden skin catching the faint moonlight, the beams highlighting all that dark hair tied back with a strip of leather. He carries himself with the easy confidence of someone who's never worried about dying, and likely never will.

His gaze skims over me, pauses, then *narrows*.

"Oh," he murmurs, more to himself than to us. "Now *that*'s interesting."

Thane sighs as he takes a step toward the newcomer—and another one that, coincidentally, takes him right in front of me. "You're trespassing, Morgane."

The other fae grins. "We're *bandits*, Aurex. Trespassing is the profession. Or have you forgotten in your old age?"

"I've seen half as many centuries as you."

"All the more reason that you should relinquish your companion to me." His eyes stay on me, his head tilting. "She's a demoness." The amber color *glows*. "An outsider. Oh, yes. I want her."

No, he fucking *doesn't*.

Sensing my sudden unease, Binx launches himself from his perch on my shoulders. He lands soundlessly on the moss, rising up on all fours, his ears arrowed back as he hisses at Morgane.

Morgane glances down at Binx, losing some of the fae's lazy amusement. "What—"

My breath catches just as Thane swoops down, so quick that he manages to grab Binx before the ungez even knows that he moved. I can sense that Binx is stunned that Thane has bundled him up against his chest, though he doesn't fight back as Thane whirls, shoving Binx at me.

I accept my soul-pet, murmuring softly so that he knows I'm okay, that he doesn't need to protect me… not when Thane is obviously willing to do it.

He's back in front of me again, bracing his legs, fingers tapping the hilt of his sword. "I found her first."

The other fae stops watching Binx with a curious tilt to his head, instead focusing on the much bigger threat.

"Aurex," he says with a laugh that reminds me of *my* fae bandit, "you know the rules. If you carry a prize worth noticing, someone's bound to ask for a look."

"And you've looked."

"Mm." Morgane hums. "And I'd like to do more than that."

I stiffen, ready to back away and get out of his sight, but Thane only rolls his shoulders, loose and unbothered.

"First blood," he says. "Or are you feeling ambitious tonight?"

Morgane laughs outright this time. "Always first blood. I'm fond of my head where I keep it, and our numbers are few as it is."

Thane nods in agreement, and as one, they both pull their swords from their sheaths.

The steel just about sings. The sound is different from anything I've ever heard before, almost musical in the motion.

Then they bow.

They actually *bow*.

"Winner keeps his prize," Morgane says cheerfully. As though they're not about to engage in a swordfight, the fae bandit is *cheerful*.

What the…

Thane lifts his sword. "And the loser pays."

"Gold?" the fae asks. "If that's all you want, Aurex, then—"

Thane's smile is slow yet undeniably threatening in its wicked curve. "You couldn't afford her, but I'll take whatever gold you're carrying when I win. Ready?"

Morgane lifts his own sword. "Always."

As they approach, something in the air shifts. I tighten my fingers in Binx's fur, unable to look away as the fight begins.

Only it's not a brawl, is it? It's a *dance*.

In Sombra, a challenge between males isn't all

that common. However, it's nothing like this. When a male demon challenges another, it's a battle between the might of their horns. They rush and they ram, and the stronger demon often wins. Whenever you see a male in Nuit with a broken horn, you're often looking at the challenge loser.

This is nothing like that.

Their swords meet in flashing arcs, steel gliding and kissing rather than crashing. Their footwork is precise, bodies turning and pivoting with effortless grace. They circle, advance, retreat… constant probing for weakness, looking for the opportunity to draw first blood and end the fight.

The other fae laughs as he attacks. "You've gone soft, Aurex!"

Thane parries smoothly. "And you've gone predictable, Morgane."

A flurry of strikes—too fast for me to follow—ends with Thane spinning aside, cloak flaring like a shadow given form.

I realize my hands are clenched. Not in fear, though. In *anticipation.*

By my ear, Binx snuffles softly, cheering Thane on. Seeing the fae male protect me from his clan… in this moment, Binx has decided that Thane's worthy of sharing me with my soul-pet, and that's more of a shock to me than what happens next.

Because even as the other fae presses him, I *know*

—deep down, all the way to my bones—who will win this fight.

A feint.

A turn.

Thane steps inside the other fae's guard, blade flashing once in a clean, decisive strike across Morgane's middle.

Golden blood sprays, arcing right at me.

It splashes across my cheek, warm and startling, and I gasp as the fae staggers back with a hiss, clutching his chest. He drops to one knee, breathing hard, but though it must hurt, it's nowhere near fatal since his head is still on the stump of his neck.

He's alive, and Thane's the victor.

Morgane looks up at Thane, bowing his head in quick understanding of that fact. A hollow laugh escapes him. "Still dangerous, I see."

Thane lowers his sword. "Lesson learned?"

After a moment, the other bandit rises, keeping his arm wrapped around the front of his torso. "For this eve." His gaze flicks to me, undeniably curious and just a touch disappointed. "Enjoy your prize, Aurex."

Then, before I can wonder if he means me or the bag of clinking gold he flings at Thane, Morgane melts into the woods as though he'd never been here at all.

I blink, stunned, trying to make sense of what just

happened. My lips part, but I can't even think of what I want to say other than, "Oh."

Hearing the soft sound, Thane turns to me immediately, leaning in close to wipe the blood from my cheek with the side of his thumb.

"You alright, demoness?"

I... I think so? "Um. Yes?"

His eyes laugh at me, his familiar amusement at the question in my voice. "You frightened?"

That's definitely one thing that I'm *not*.

I shake my head, heart racing. "No."

"Good."

Thane backs away, looking at the gold blood shimmering on the length of his blade. Reaching beneath his cloak, he pulls some sort of rag out of somewhere, wiping away the blood before returning the sword to its sheath.

Only then do I find the words to ask him something that seems super obvious to me: "Why would he challenge you? If he knows you, he'd have to know you'd win."

Thane's eyes seem to flash in the moonlight as they meet mine.

"Because you don't have any idea how much you're worth in a realm like this," he says darkly as my breath stutters. "And because," he adds softly, "I won't let anyone take what's mine."

Mine? I'm his?

"Thane—"

"Good work," he says, turning away from me. "Now if only I can take the gold of everyone who comes after us, I can finally retire from being a bandit."

Oh.

Oh.

Godsdamn it.

HE MIGHT NOT MIND, BUT WE DON'T GET FAR BEFORE we run into trouble *again.*

This time, I'm ready for it. I refuse to let Thane distract me, especially now that I understand just how dangerous this fae world is. I'm listening closely, and even if I'm not, my soul-pet is up for the duty.

Binx had gone still when the goldcaps first attacked, and he jumped down, darting forward when the fae bandit appeared to challenge Thane. Sure, Thane handed him back to me to keep him safe, but Binx is still determined to protect me. That's why, when he hisses, then leaps again, landing right in front of me, I instantly pause, searching for the latest threat.

It's another bandit. Like Morgane, he doesn't last long; like Morgane, Thane expects his gold if he proves to be the better swordsman. Thane sizes him up once Yarrow agrees, then stalks toward him. I'm not sure about the hierarchy among these marauders, but Thane doesn't even draw his sword this time. He lunges for the other bandit, disarming him with a quick twist of his wrist and a look sharp enough to make the fae reconsider every single one of his life's choices.

The other bandit retreats after passing over his pouch of gold, muttering curses in a language that I *don't* understand, but I don't need to. It's pretty obvious what he was saying.

I finally asked how we can communicate; since it's not courtesy of the essence that I'm struggling to hold onto, it has to be something else. It is. As it turns out, Noctavara—being a fae realm branched off from Faerie—once had rifts that were open to countless worlds. An early settler casted a spell that created a universal tongue. Once you step onto this plane, the magic takes hold, and even though it's only the slavers that come and go from Noctavara these days, the spell still works, though the fae have their own dialects they can slip into if they choose to.

Since Thane prefers to tease me in the common tongue, I don't worry about it. Besides, I have to wonder what other types of magic are native to this world. Though we've barely met, Thane looks right through my curiosity. No, he tells me, the realm itself isn't dampening my shadow powers.

So who is? In answer to that, I get another one of those twisted responses that leaves me more confused, but distracted enough that Thane can move ahead, escaping my constant questions.

It lasts until he has to dispatch another fae monster—a troll, he explains, after he lops off its head and the creature turns to stone—before he finally thins his lips while looking at me.

At my *horns*.

"Right," he says. "I was hoping it wouldn't come to this, but they're going to be a problem."

I arch a brow. "That's nice, but they're attached."

"I noticed."

"I'd like them to stay attached."

Hint, hint. If he thinks that he's going to use his sword to remove my horns so that I pass more easily for a fae female and the Noctavaran locals finally stop treating me like an outsider, that's not going to happen. They may be tiny nubs, but they're mine, and I'm not getting rid of them when he swears we should be out of the Shadowed Woods in the next day or two.

At my feet, Binx bounds over to Thane, batting at the hem of his cloak.

Ignoring the ungez, he steps closer to me, fingers already lifting. Since he doesn't have his sword out, I don't knee him in the cock.

"This won't hurt."

It better not.

Magic brushes my skin. It's cool, light, *precise*. The air shimmers with gold, and as it fades, suddenly the familiar weight at my temples is gone.

I reach up instinctively, groping for my horns, and finding nothing.

They're not there. Hidden somehow, I guess. The illusion seamless enough that even *I* almost believe it.

Glamour, I think. Thane used fae glamour to hide my horns.

"They won't see them," he confirms. "Most fae here won't look twice if you pass for one of us. You have the pointed ears, and your shadows are barely visible. That should keep some of the worst away."

"I'm proud of who I am," I say. "I don't need to hide."

He meets my eyes. "You do if you don't want attention. In Noctavara, attention is dangerous."

Everything in this fae world seems to be too dangerous…

With a sigh, I let my hand fall. Binx rubs against my ankle, letting me know that he doesn't mind my missing horns. I blow him a soft kiss that has Thane frowning.

We walk in silence for a while after that.

When this part of the woods opens onto a wider clearing that makes it easier for us to spot any prospective threats, Thane stops. He studies me for a moment—really studies me—then exhales like he's made a decision.

Suddenly, the glamour lifts. The weight returns, and so do my horns.

I glance at him. "You didn't have to remove the spell."

"I know."

"So why did you?"

His mouth tilts into something that isn't quite a smile. "Because I like looking at the real you, demoness."

Unbidden, heat curls low in my stomach. The bond stretching between us becomes a tangible thing, and I find myself stepping toward Thane before I catch myself and dig my boots into the dirt.

"Really?"

He jerks his head, a silent assent, before he looks away from me. Running his fingers through his dark curls, he clears his throat. "We should keep moving. If I sense someone near, I'll pull the glamour back together. Until then, pay attention."

Oh, I promise you, I will.

As he lopes away, Binx brushes against my leg, too smug for an ungez.

"Hush," I murmur.

He clicks his fangs.

"I know, I know. But I can't worry about that now."

I can't worry about the way Thane is reacting to me. My horns… he likes my horns. He likes seeing the real me enough to drop the glamour when we're alone. He doesn't know why he's drawn to me yet, but it's undeniable that—in some way—he is.

And somehow, that feels more dangerous than the blade at my throat ever did.

As has become our habit, the three of us walk in silence for a while after that.

The forest no longer feels *that* hostile. Even without the glamour to shield me, we've entered a stretch where no one attacks us, thank the gods (even if I can't thank my fae companion). Thane says it's because the two bandits he battled would've warned any other locals to give us a wide berth. Even the monsters in the woods keep their distance as evening falls, so we should be safe once we settle down for the night.

That's coming soon, once Thane finds a spot that he trusts. I'm ready to find a safe tree to rest against, but as we go on, I just can't shake the awareness of dried blood on my skin. It itches. Smells weird; almost metallic. It flakes off a little, and I use my claw to get rid of some of it, but nowhere near enough.

As if I needed *another* reminder that I'm not home. In Sombra, shadow magic would've already cleaned it away. Even though I don't have two distinct forms, I'm made up of enough shadows to freshen up without taking a bath.

Here, the dirt clings. I'm sure I stink from all of the walking, and there's a slight tear in my skirts from where I snagged them on a branch to go with the one on my sleeve. I'd give anything to be indoors… except sacrifice Rafe, that is. Which means that, until I find him, I'm stuck following a fae bandit, and that means I have to make *other* sacrifices.

But bathing? That's not one of them.

"I need to wash," I say finally.

Thane glances at me. "There's no bathhouse nearby."

After sleeping outside last night and watching him kill a clan of goldcaps *and* a troll, I wasn't expecting anything like that. Luckily, when it comes to bathing outside, that's something I'm used to. "I don't need a bathhouse."

That gets a smile out of him. "I know a place."

<hr>

The Noctavara lake reveals itself without warning, a silvered bowl cradled by dark trees that lean inward as if to guard it. Moonlight—or sunlight, I'm not sure in the Shadowed Woods—spills across the water in a slow, steady sheen, turning the surface into glass. It's still without a single ripple to mar it.

More than that, it feels old, and that's saying something coming from a Sombra demon.

I slow without meaning to, my boots sinking slightly into the damp earth at the shore. The air is cool here, beaded with moisture, carrying the faint mineral scent of stone and water. My shadows loosen around my ankles, drifting lazily as if even they are relieved to have found a place to rest.

Binx hops down from my shoulder, padding to the edge to peer at his reflection, white eyes glowing faintly in the dark.

"I need to get clean," I say, more to the lake than to Thane. Between the mud from sleeping in the moss, the blood, and the lingering grit of travel, my skin feels too tight, too dirty.

Thane hums softly somewhere behind me, the sound thoughtful. "You couldn't find a better spot in the woods than here."

I glance back at him. While I approached the lake with Binx, he hung at the entrance to the clearing.

"I'm going to make sure it's clear," he says, answering my wordless question. "Go on, Alana. I'll be right back."

I don't know if I should be offended or grateful that Thane found an excuse to allow me to strip out of my boots and my dress without an audience. As my mate, he should want to see me naked; as a male, he should take the excuse if I were willing to let him. Was I? I… don't know.

Still, he's giving me some privacy, and desperate as I am to scrub up, I take it. I shuck off my dress, folding it neatly and leaving it near Binx. The ungez immediately adopts a guarding position, plopping his furry butt on top of my bodice. I kick my boots next to him, careful not to disturb Binx, then wade into the lake.

Compared to the lava pools, the lake is filled with ice. I don't mind it. I've been feeling a little flushed since I watched Thane's skill with his sword up close and personal, and if I use the excuse of the fae bandit's blood splashed across my face to dunk under the surface, that's okay. Hey. I really did need to get clean.

So consumed with using my claws to get rid of the blood spray, I don't realize that Thane's returned until Binx yowls, catching my attention.

I glance up to see that Thane's already unfastening his sword belt, his movements easy, practiced, like a male who has bathed in strange places more times than he can count. He's still dressed, but as our eyes meet, I know instantly that he plans on taking advantage of our trip to the lake to wash up himself.

I'm treading the water, letting it come up to my breasts. All Thane can see is my damp hair, my horns, and a slightly stunned expression as I watch him with my lips parted.

My mate is getting undressed.

My mate is getting naked.

My mate—

I dunk a little lower, hoping the cool water will do something—*anything*—to cool me off.

The first time I saw a male naked, it was Rafe. Of course it was. We were still spawn, barely a handful of years old, and I was amazed by what he had hanging between his legs. I squealed, asked if all males had handles, and grabbed it before he could get out of my reach.

Rafe cried and ran to Kennedy to snitch on me. When she finally understood what had her son so upset, she snickered and went right to my house to share the story with Mom. Needless to say, I didn't get in *trouble* trouble, though Mom did remind me that good halflings kept their claws to themselves.

Much later, when I realized that I'd basically tried to yank poor Rafe's cock off before I knew better, I was so humiliated. Rafe, being Rafe, just looked at me hopefully and asked if I wanted to try again.

Males.

Now, I know there are plenty in Nuit who hope that, one day, Rafe and I will open our eyes and realize that we were meant for each other. Look past our friendship and decide to deepen it into something *more*. Mom would be thrilled; so would Kennedy. But that was never going to happen even before Rafe fell head over horns for Katrin, or I met Thane and realized that I was meant for *him*.

And, unless I figure out a way to stop him, I'm about to see what Thane Aurex looks like naked.

Only… do I want to stop him?

I should. I know I should. And yet, the most I can do is call out an offer: "If you want, I can turn my back until you're in the lake."

Thane snorts. "We've been traveling in close quarters. Eventually, you'll see me out of my clothes." Even from a distance, I can see the way his eyes gleam. "Besides, I already saw you."

My cheeks flame. "A good and honorable male wouldn't remind me of that."

His grin is wicked as he slips off his cloak. In the next moment, his top is gone, silver moonlight kissing bare golden skin, giving me a perfect view of lean muscle and quiet strength. "Ah, but I'm a bandit, Alana of Sombra. And bandits aren't known for being honorable, are they?"

Though they're under the water, I cross my arms over my breasts. "So why should I continue to let you accompany Binx and me on our hunt for Rafe if you're such a rogue?"

Besides the fact that, if I hadn't, I'd be dead countless times over already. The goldcaps, the troll… they weren't trying to capture me. Oh, no. They wanted to end my existence, killing me before the second prophecy has the chance.

"Because I'd just follow behind you anyway," is his answer as he kicks off one boot, then the other. "Understand this, demoness. I'm not doing this out of the kindness of my heart. While you're in the Shadowed Woods, you're a target. My fellow bandits will come after you the same way I did."

I suck in a breath as Thane briskly shoves his pants down, adding them to the pile of his discarded clothing.

Unaware of how he's affecting me, Thane steps into the water, the lake parting around him. I keep my eyes carefully fixed on the far bank, trying not to peek at his delectable body any more than I already have. But, well, I'm only (part) human. I can't help myself, and my mouth goes dry as I take in the golden cock dangling invitingly between his legs.

As though he can sense my hungry stare from halfway across the lake, he takes his time before plunging into the water. When he resurfaces, he shakes his head, sending the water flying everywhere, his dark curls plastered to his forehead.

I swallow the nervous lump lodged in my throat. "So this is all about gold?"

Thane chuckles, the sound carrying all the way to me. "It's always about gold."

Of course. Well, that explains why he hasn't left my side yet. Not because he feels the same pull toward me that I feel for him, but because he's a mercenary all the way to the depths of his shadowed heart.

Worse, he's a charming bandit who is oblivious to the fact that I'm mere demon's lengths away, and I'm *naked*…

I try not to let my disappointment show. It's become clear to me that Thane is like the humans of Earth: he has no idea that he's meant to be the one true mate of a halfling demoness. And, well, I'm not about to tell him. Not yet. Not until I've saved Rafe and I can look at what my future will be like after that.

Besides, Stevie and Corbin have known they are mates for three gold moons now. If they've managed to hold off on bonding for that long, I can wait until Rafe is safe and back in Sombra.

And who's to say that I want to take a fae bandit as my mate? The gods have given him to me, but if they've made a mistake, I can accept that and move on myself. Sure, I wouldn't have that elusive fated mate to hope for, as we only get one, but there are plenty of males in Sombra who might suit me better. All I have to do is share my essence with one, then finalize a bond through mating, and I would be his for eternity as he would be mine.

Having Thane near is a tease to my senses—especially my eyes as I watch the water cling to his skin, remembering the quick glimpse I got of him completely unclothed—but if it's all about gold… at least that's a reasoning I can understand. It's a selfish one, triggered by greed, but if that means I can trust him enough… fine.

"A dead demoness can't help you swindle your fellow bandits," I remark.

"Exactly." There's a triumphant note to his voice as he runs his fingers through his curls. "I'm so glad you see it my way. Maybe then you'll stop doubting my swordsmanship. I'll keep you safe, and if you end up with blood spattered on you, there's always another stream or lake where we can bathe."

Oh, goody. More times where I'll be around my one true mate naked.

If only I were the type of halfling to resist temptation…

I have to. I *have* to. And if that means I stay as far away from Thane as I can, busying myself with finishing my bath, then waiting until he's dressed again and making another circle to see if anyone's come close before I scurry from the water… that's exactly what I do.

For Rafe.

For… Rafe.

Godsdamn it. Where is he?

THE RUSH OF BATHING WITH THANE—EVEN WITH THE distance between us—wears off as my worry for Rafe only grows. I want to believe that he's okay. That whoever has him is keeping him safe… for now. After the way the goldcaps attacked us with a frenzy, then the bandits challenged Thane, I can't deny just how dangerous the Shadowed Woods are.

Not to mention my feelings for my bandit…

Whatever happens after, I'm determined to save Rafe first. That's why I suggest we keep on going after we're both ready to move on, but he insists that we look for a place for us to rest.

How can I argue? My slice is gone, and I'm sure Thane's healed, too, but I can't imagine engaging in *four* different fights has left him with enough energy to continue.

So I agree, and before I know it, he's gesturing beneath another tree just like the one I slept under last night. I share a pouch of dried meat and thin crackers with Binx. Thane has his own, and we both finish off the last of our canteens that we refilled at the lake before we left.

Murmuring that he'll get more water in the morning, he collects my canteen, attaches them both to his sword belt, then removes his cloak.

"For you."

I nod, a wordless show of gratitude.

Look, Mom. I'm getting better.

I figure Thane is going to climb up and take his perch now that our supper is done. To my surprise, he plops down next to me, kicking his legs out in front of him. Folding his hands behind his head, his gaze searches for the spattering of stars peeking through the late evening sky.

Still glancing skyward, he says, "You're very determined to get this demon of yours back."

My heart stutters, my worry for Rafe jumping the way it does whenever Thane mentions him. But, like always, he doesn't use his name—calling him my 'demon' or my 'friend'—and that bothers me for some reason.

"Rafe," I tell him. "His name is Rafe."

"That his true name?"

It's the only one he has. "He is Rafe of Sombra, spawn of Loki and Kennedy."

Thane nods. "Rafe, then. He that important to you?"

"Yes."

Finally, he looks my way. "He's not your lover. You said that. Do you want him to be?"

The question is casual. *Too* casual.

I'm not the only one who notices. Binx had already made himself a nest in the skirts of my dress, cozying up now that he's full. As though he can sense the direction the conversation between Thane and me has gone in, he lifts his chin off of his paws, twitching his ears slightly as a sliver of his white eyes peeks through.

I stroke his head, then tell Thane firmly, "No."

He hums. "Could he be your mate, then?"

My heart nearly skips a beat to hear Thane murmur that word.

Mate.

Maaaatttee.

"No," I say, and this time I choose my next words carefully. "He's just my friend. My very close friend." I look him dead in the eye. "Family, but he is *not* my mate."

Thane studies me for a moment longer, like he's trying to decide if that answers the question he asked, and ones he kept to himself.

Then he exhales. "Strange thing, devotion."

"Why's that?"

He shrugs. "We don't have it here. Not like that."

"Devotion?" I echo.

"The bonds you were telling me about," he corrects. "Fated ones, what you have with Binx, plus this friendship you have with Rafe of Sombra. See, Noctavara was cursed long before I was born. No one here has any sort of bonded partner." He folds his legs in, resting an arm leisurely around his knees. "Not unless they steal one."

"How do you know that?" I ask.

He gives a small, crooked smile. "Because if we did, we wouldn't need slavers."

I swallow, then, because I can't help myself, I ask, "And you? Do you have a lover?"

He shakes his head. "Nah. Not me. Not now."

It's the truth. Even if I didn't know that the fae can't lie, I feel the honesty as it plucks at our bond like it's a string.

"Thane—"

He pushes himself up to his feet. "I should head up and be look-out. Sleep tight, Alana of Sombra. Tomorrow we push harder to find your friend."

As I watch Thane shimmy easily up the tree, I bite down on my bottom lip.

I don't tell him what I know. I don't tell him about the pull I feel toward him, or ask if maybe he feels the same for me. I don't tell him that he has to be able to bond because both Fate and the gods have given him to me… and I tell myself none of that matters.

For now, only Rafe does.

Everything else can wait.

I t's been four moons in Noctavara—four nights where I sleep under the stars… and beneath Thane's perch in the tree he chooses for the eve —and there's still no sign of Rafe.

On the plus side, we've finally reached the end of the Shadowed Woods with only one more challenge from a fellow bandit. There was another swarm of guldcaps that Thane eliminated, two more trolls, and a kelpie that would've attempted to drown me in one of the mirrored lakes if Binx didn't nip at my heels, warning me away from the creature, before Thane sent it away with a command in the old Faerie language I can't understand.

Now, I don't think I would've *died*, but spending the rest of eternity as the captive of a creature that was a mix between a mortal horse and fish didn't seem like a good time to me…

Thane warns that the dangers don't end just because the dark Shadowed Woods give way to a bright forest that gleams with gold. From the gold-tinged leaves fluttering on metallic branches to a sky that's a mix of magenta and burnished gold swirls, plus a sun that actually looks like the one from Earth instead of the constant silver moon that shone over the Shadowed Woods… it's exactly what I imagined a fae forest to look like, especially since the monarch butterflies seem more at home here when they inevitably reappear.

They don't stay long, and whenever Thane edges out of the woods, finding the main road that's designated for the traders and other caravans, they disappear completely. I almost think that he does that on purpose, as though he's trying to avoid the butterflies. Since the golden forest means that we're one step closer to reaching the Gilded Court, that's fine with me.

At the same time, he's careful to guide us back into the thick trees where we're out of sight of any travelers. He still puts the glamour over my horns whenever he senses someone—or something—coming too close, but more often than not, it's just a fae bandit, a travelworn halfling, and Binx, who is having the time of his life bounding around the golden forest, sniffing the plants, and trying to eat the strange fruit growing on the trees no matter how many times I have to warn him that he'll be trapped in Noctavara forever if he does.

Only once my ungez understands that he'll be trapped here *without me* does he scamper up Thane's leg, nosing the pouch that stores his dried meat so that he can have a snack.

It's only been four moons, but it feels like forever. Like I've known Thane forever. Even Binx has decided he's not so bad, though I can't tell if my mate bond with Thane is affecting the soulbond I have with my soul-pet. It's possible, but damn if it isn't sweet, seeing Binx get along with Thane.

I want to flag down travelers and ask if they've heard anything about slavers visiting demon realms and returning with outsiders. Considering they had been in Brille Rouge, prepared to bring Katrin and her kin back with them only to settle for Rafe when his barrier saved the demonesses, it seems like a very common occurrence.

Of course, Thane points out that, if I accept that demons and demonesses fetch a high price in Noctavara, all it would take is a more powerful fae seeing through his glamour for me to be snagged next. So far, he considers me his; after the amount of gold coin he earned from other marauders challenging him, I *am* worth a lot. Recognizing that, I asked him point-blank if he was going to sell me to earn more now that we've left the Shadowed Woods behind us.

He laughed, said 'why would I do that', and

surged forward to check out a concerning sound long before I realized that he didn't answer me.

That's what he does. When he doesn't want to answer a question—and he can't lie—he gives me a non-answer. Like when I asked him how old he was after Morgane's comment had me wondering. Dad was more than ten centuries old when he mated Mom, and I've always known that once a spawn matures—and that happens at about two decades for halflings versus two centuries for demons—a mate of any age is appropriate so long as they're immortal.

To my surprise, Thane revealed that he wasn't even that old. A hundred-and-fifty fae years, with the last two decades spent as a fae bandit staking out his corner of the Shadowed Woods and earning as much gold as possible.

I didn't bother asking about his fixation with the metal. He changes the subject every time, and I knew it wasn't worth it.

However, I did ask, "What did you do before that?," because I… I want to know everything about my mate that I can before the essence exchange ruins all the fun.

He'd smiled and just said, "Nothing half as interesting."

I still don't know what that means.

I'm not the only one who asks questions. He seeds them into normal conversation, but I finally notice that he's interested in my relationship with Rafe, what it's like living in Sombra, and how exactly my shadow magic works. He wants to know about my soulbond with Binx, though he's careful to never mention mate bonds around me after his admission that the fae are cursed to never form them on their own.

I'm sure he's wrong. He has to be. He's on the other end of *my* bond, but I'm not ready to tell him that. Not yet. Instead, I answer his questions as best I can, throwing back some of my own, and keep on moving forward until he tells us it's once again time to settle down for the night.

Until this eve. Until Thane sees that I'm dragging more than usual, that I flinch a little when he says that we should start searching for a safe place to rest, and he pauses.

And then he says five magic words that nearly have me genuflecting in front of him the way that Corbin did when he first met Stevie:

"Want to find an inn?"

THE INN THAT THANE LEADS BINX AND ME INTO IS older than it looks at first glance. Makes sense. This is a fae world full of immortals, and like Sombra, you often get the feeling that—with so much time for its inhabitants—it's almost frozen in it.

Its timbers lean inward, the dark wood polished smooth by centuries of travelers who came through

Noctavara. A low fire burns in the hearth, casting warm light over rough tables filled with wary faces. Most of them are covered in cloaks like the one Thane wears. Others have softly glowing golden skin, but nowhere near the level of beauty and refinement that he has. In fae realms, there are high fae—the nobles—and low fae—the tradesmen, the seamstresses, the farmers, and the slavers. This inn serves as a tavern for the low fae, and one that Thane has used when he had a coin to spare for a night indoors, where the inn keeps rooms on the second story.

The way I see it, his pouch is a lot fuller because of me. He can buy my supper in the kitchen below, plus a soft bed upstairs for me to sleep on, and I won't even feel like I need to 'thank you'. If only for the night, I want to pretend I'm back home with all the amenities I'm used to.

So consumed with looking around, it takes me a moment to notice that all conversation began to falter the moment our trio stepped inside.

Not all at once. Not so dramatically that it's undeniable. But I feel it: the subtle shift, the pause between words, the flicker of curious attention that hits us before bounding away again before they're caught.

Thane feels it, too.

As our guide, he'd walked in first to make sure it was safe. Now? He moves to my side, taking a step away. His hand finds the small of my back, firm and deliberate, fingers pressing through fabric. He's making it clear that, no matter what, I'm with him.

Kind of like he's claiming me…

With Binx on my shoulder and Thane keeping his hand there, he jerks his chin at the end of the room. There's a counter with a gorgeous fae female leaning forward, showing off her bosom. She has the Noctavaran coloring, from her amber eyes to her golden skin, though her hair is the color of honey. It falls in loose curls around her pointed ears, making me all the more aware that my hair's been a tangled mess since I first arrived in this world.

She's stunning, and I tighten up as Thane makes a beeline right for her. Does he know her? Does he think she's pretty? What is he—

"Innkeeper," he says, warm voice friendly enough without being *too* friendly. "We need two rooms for the night."

The innkeeper's eyes dart to me, though she never loses her welcoming smile. Then she's glancing where my horns usually are; they're glamoured, barely noticeable unless you know what to look for. Then, lastly, to Binx, who peers out from my shoulder with glowing white eyes and a deceptively innocent expression.

"I'm afraid there's only one room left for the night," the innkeeper says after a moment. "With one bed."

One bed… for the three of us?

I open my mouth, ready to argue, but Thane speaks first.

"That's even better."

***

UP CLOSE, THE BED THE INNKEEPER LED US TO upstairs looks even smaller.

It's too narrow. Too *intimate*. The walls of the cozy seem to press in, the single window shuttered tight against the golden woods beyond it. A fire is glowing, bathing us with warmth, and highlighting the single wood-hewn nightstand until it's more gold than dark.

Beside us, the innkeeper murmurs that there's fresh baked bread and gnome stew for supper if we'd like some sent up to our room before pointing out the facilities down the hall in case we want to freshen up.

It irks me that her gaze shoots my way when she adds that part, but Thane quickly confirms that we'll head down ourselves to try the cook's famed stew before we turn in for the eve. Then, making it clear that that was a dismissal, he waits until she leaves to close the door behind her.

Now it's just us, and though we've been traveling in close quarters for our fifth moon now, I've never been so intimately aware of Thane Aurex before.

"I can take the floor," I blurt out, because I am *not* weak and I am *not* helpless and I am *definitely* not swooning just because he's removed his cloak and is currently rolling his shoulders like he can't wait to lie down on that bed.

Thane turns to me slowly. "No," he says, gentle yet unyielding. "You won't."

Something in his tone stills me.

"But—"

"We're out of the woods now," he continues. "The low fae have a tendency to talk. They watch. I'd hoped that the innkeeper would insist we take one room because I couldn't let you out of my sight, Alana, but I didn't want to unnerve you. I'll take the floor, but I won't leave you alone. As it is, if there are already rumors spreading through Noctavara, I don't intend to feed them any further."

"Rumors," I echo. "What kind of rumors?"

"I spoke with Morgane last night while you were asleep—"

"He challenged you again?"

Thane shakes his head. "Not quite. It's our bandit code. He knows I have you. He knows I've won you. That's why, when he heard talk of a shadow demon traveling under glamour… of slavers asking questions and soldiers listening… he told me. That's why the inn was safer for us tonight. They'd never expect Thane Aurex would bring his shadow demon prize to this inn."

The way the fae on the first floor watched him as closely as they did Binx and me, I get the feeling that he's as well-known in this part of the realm as he is in the Shadowed Woods.

"And you?" I ask. "What do they say about you?"

"That I'm trouble," he answers without any hesitation. Then, a hint softer, "And that anything under my protection is off-limits."

Protection.

He doesn't say *mine* again. He doesn't need to. Whatever the other fae think when they see us together, it's clear he's continuing to stake his claim on me.

At supper, he keeps me close; too close to be coincidence. His arm drapes behind my chair, his presence a shield I didn't realize I'd been leaning into until I try to straighten on my wooden seat and I can't.

Binx wedges his shadowy body between us on the bench, tail flicking lazily, eyes never quite closing. If anyone wonders if I'm a shadow demon, my soul-pet might give me away, but Binx refuses to stay up in the room without us. Thane makes a point to mention off-handedly that Binx is a creature we brought with us from the Shadowed Woods, letting the golden fae form their own conclusions.

It's true. We did bring Binx out of the Shadowed Woods—only because I led him into them in the first place.

When supper is done, we return to the room to find that the fire in the hearth has burned low.

Shadows pool along the walls, familiar and strange all at once.

Thane waits.

That, more than anything, unravels me.

He doesn't reach for me. Doesn't crowd me. He simply watches as I move, as I unlace my boots, as I hesitate before leaving my dress in place.

"You can sleep," he says quietly. "I'll be right here. You're safe with me, Alana."

Of course I am, and I know I'm being ridiculous. This male is my mate. It's one thing for him to climb up in a tree to have a better vantage point in the woods. To make him lie down on the floor while I take the only bed just isn't right.

"You're right. The bed is small, but if we squeeze, we can both fit. That way no one is on the floor."

I expect my fae bandit to show his gentlemanly side and refuse my offer. When he doesn't, staying quiet instead of outright rejecting me, it hits me that he must be as exhausted as I am from our constant travel.

"Please," I add. It's not a 'thank you', but it's close, and I watch for his reaction before I tack on, "I insist."

Thane tracks his fingers through his curls, a shadowed look on his beautiful face. "Are you sure?"

I'm nervous, and I make it a tease: "If you can handle the stink from traveling, then yes."

He chuckles under his breath. "I'm sure it's no worse than mine."

Bullshit. One of my Mom's favorite Human expressions, but it's never been more apt. Whether it's a fae thing or a Thane thing, it doesn't matter. He has that same spicy masculine scent that drives me wild. This closer, I'd almost prefer him to stink of a feral demon, of brimstone and acrid smoke, because then I wouldn't start thinking about giving in to temptations again…

"Sleep," I tell Thane. "Or don't. But I mean it. I'll feel like crud if you choose to take the floor after I offered."

Then, I climb onto the bed carefully, stiff with total awareness that he's watching me move. After a moment, Thane follows, sitting on the edge at first— near enough that I feel the heat of him, the slow, steady rhythm of his breath—before he eases his body back.

No. He lies in his side. Facing away from me, but still so close, I can breathe in his scent without him noticing.

I turn toward the wall, heart pounding far too hard for sleep to come easily. Binx climbs in between us, warm and solid, and I close my eyes.

I must have fallen asleep. Since I'm suddenly awak again, I know had to have been asleep. How long was I out for? No idea, but it was long enough for me to come to with a start and notice two very important things.

The first one? Fluttering open my eyes, I see a single monarch butterfly perched on the end of my nose.

I jump once I notice it, scurrying back before I pull myself up into a seated position. The butterfly flaps its orange-and-black wings, fluttering away from me as my heart damn near beats its way out of my chest. Even in Sombra, the faripoz don't interrupt my sleep.

Maybe it was a good thing, though. Because the second thing I notice?

Is that the bed is empty. So is the room. And the fire is dead…

I jolt up. Thane is gone. No Binx, either. And the door? It stands open just a crack, letting in enough light that when the shadow in the corner moves, I see it.

I open my mouth.

"Don't scream," a voice murmurs, smooth and unfamiliar. "I'm not here to harm you, demoness, but the queen has questions."

My breath catches. I don't know what's worse: that he knows what I am despite the glamour I can sense near my forehead, or that he's here because of the queen.

Oh. I know what's worse: it's the sound of boots scuffing against the floor, the flash of light reflecting off of the sword the cloaked male carries easily, like he's never without it.

Soldier, I think. And somewhere in the pit of my chest… the bond or something else… it tightens, not from fear, but in the certainty that Thane will come. I don't know where he is, where he's gone, and what happened to Binx, but I sense them both on the other end of each bond and know that they'll come for me if they can.

The soldier takes three purposeful steps toward me, but he never gets the chance to take a fourth. The door slams open hard enough to rattle the walls, and the shadows *move*.

Not mine. *Theirs.*

Binx streaks in first. A flash of black and white, all teeth and fury as he launches himself straight at the hidden soldier. The fae shouts, staggering back before whipping around, and that's when Thane appears in the doorway, his sword already in motion.

There's no flourish, no warning. He simply follows Binx into the room, pivots once, and drives the blade clean through the soldier's neck, taking his head with one strike.

Gold blood sprays *everywhere*.

It paints the wall. It spatters the floor. A few warm

drops hit my cheek, but I'm too stunned—halfway lost in a dream that's turned into a nightmare—to do more than dab at it with my fingertips.

That's when I make another mistake. I think that it's over. That, for whatever reason the queen sent her soldier after me, she only sent one.

And then Thane turns to me.

For half a heartbeat, I see it—the open worry, the raw fury, something dangerously close to *panic*—and then he's moving again, crossing the room in three long strides.

His hand closes around my upper arm. "There will be others coming, but we won't be here for them to find. We're leaving," he says. "Now."

Binx had dropped down before the fae's body fell. Now he leaps onto the bed, bounding to my other side, shadows flaring as he turns and snarls at the door, daring anyone else to try. Thane yanks me out of bed, then forward, hauling me through the hall, down the stairs, past startled faces and half-risen patrons who are too slow, too shocked, or too smart to intervene as he drags me into the kitchen where a drowsy cook stirs something in a pot.

A male voice yells behind us, making the cook jump. "Someone get the guards—"

Thane kicks the back door open.

Cold night air slams into us, and the golden light of Noctavara in the early morning hours welcomes us like an old friend.

My mate doesn't slow, and because of that, neither do Binx and me. My ungez bounds forward, darting around my ankles, keeping up with us while also determined to prove to himself that I'm all right.

Thane, it seems, feels the need to do the same.

He leads me off the road, into the golden trees, his grip never loosening even as muffled shouts follow us. I stumble once—twice—and each time he adjusts without looking, pulling me closer, shielding me with his body as though that's the most natural thing in the world for him to do.

Only when the inn is far behind us… when the sounds of pursuit fade into nothing but the hush of the forest waking up in a way better manner than I did… only then does he finally stop.

He turns on me, hands going to my shoulders, amber eyes burning in the dusk. "I *knew* it. They came for you," he says, his voice suddenly tight. "It was more than just rumors. They had *orders*."

"How do you—"

"The innkeeper warned me they were near," he bites out. "I went to check… Binx followed after me to see what I was up to… and the soldier snuck up. Near! She let him in!"

If the innkeeper still has her head after that, I'd be surprised. That's how furious Thane is… and I wish I understood it.

I wish I understood any of this.

"But why?" is all I manage to get out.

Thane exhales roughly, closing the last of the space between us, his forehead dropping to mine for only a few seconds. Just long enough for me to feel the tremor in him before he purposely drops the glamour magic, sliding his smooth skin along the edge of my horn.

"For the shadow demoness," he murmurs in a ragged voice, his fury banked as he tells me in a raw whisper: "For the one the queen wants brought to her alive."

What?

Sensing my shock, Thane pulls away enough that I can see his expression. His jaw is set, his gaze fierce. "But I won't let them take you," he adds, still deathly quiet. "We'll get your demon, no matter what it takes, but if you go before Queen Celeste, it won't be in chains, Alana of Sombra. I promise you that."

And as my mate makes his vow—as I see the true male behind the charming fae mask that is even more irresistible—the bond between us grows infinitely stronger.

Whether he knows it or not, Thane Aurex made his own version of the mate's promise to me.

I won't let them take you…

He didn't. He saved me in time, with Binx at his heels, and then fled through the woods before the soldiers could follow us. Once he realized how much he gave away, he dons that same charming demeanor as easily as he slips on his cloak, then says he's going to scout ahead. I know what he's doing. He's giving himself a moment to recover, and doing the same for me.

He'll be right back. I know he will. If there's one thing I've learned, if Thane Aurex considers you under his protection, you're *protected*. Mom's going to love him—if I ever get the chance to go back to Sombra and introduce them. I'm not worried about that now. Nope, my much bigger concern is why Queen Celeste is picking on this shadow demon halfling in particular.

Once Binx scurries around me, sniffing wildly, making sure that I'm in one piece, I crouch down by my ungez and have a quick (and silent) chat where Binx confirms everything Thane had said. Not that I doubted him. He can't lie to me, and even if he *could*, the way he grabbed me like that… he was almost as scared as I was.

By the time he does return a few moments later, my fear has hardened into resolve. I wait for him to confirm that there isn't anyone around that he can see or hear before I perch my hands on my hips and tell him, "I don't want that to happen again."

Thane looks up from where he's stopped to finally clean the dried blood from his blade. His lips quirk into a smile that doesn't quite meet his eyes. "You'd prefer fewer decapitations?"

"I'd prefer to know how to stop someone before it gets that far."

I can't always rely on Thane to save me. In that split second as the soldier started for me, I didn't even try to do anything more than scream. That's unacceptable. I've been here for five moons. If I want to make it to six, I need to be able to protect myself.

Even in Sombra, I took the protection of Mom, Dad, and the clan for granted. I was the child of prophecy; of course they would keep me safe. Here in

Noctavara, I'm just Alana of Sombra, and nothing is going to stop me from getting Rafe back.

Hey, I was bold enough to flippantly say 'tell them that I'm coming' my first eve here. Well, now they know, and I have to be prepared for other soldiers to come after me.

And if they do? I want to know how to *end* them.

Thane studies me for a long moment, something thoughtful flickering behind his guarded eyes. Then he reaches under his cloak and, seconds later, draws out a sword.

It can't be his since he set his down by his foot when he grabbed the second one. It doesn't look like Thane's sword, either. It's smaller and cleaner. Definitely sharp and well cared for.

New.

My brows lift. "You stole that? When did you steal that?"

"First of all, demoness, I didn't steal it. I paid for it."

I blink. *Paid…* "But… you're a *bandit.*"

"Still am," he agrees. "A sword like this should cost at least fifty gold coins. I got away with only having to give Morgane five for his spare. If that's not a robbery, I don't know what is."

That throws me. "You bought it from Morgane? But I thought… don't you just want to get as much gold as possible?"

"Yes, but I'm also trying to keep you alive," he

replies. "Seemed a fair investment to me, especially since I'm getting to know you, Alana of Sombra. To understand you. I assumed you'd want a sword of your own eventually."

He knows me, and he didn't even have to take my essence to figure me out. "Thane…"

My fae mate holds it out, hilt first. "On one condition."

"What is it?"

"You let me teach you how to use it."

WAS IT THAT OBVIOUS THAT I DIDN'T KNOW HOW TO wield a sword? Considering how he found me hanging from a snare trap, he already had a pretty good assessment of my survival skills. They're terrible. I never needed to develop them. In Sombra, my magic makes me powerful, and my kinship with the shadows at the end of Nuit allows me a safety among the beasts that none of my clansmen have. Besides, if I even tried to borrow Glaine's sword, Mom's head would probably burst into flames.

But I'm determined, and so is Thane.

Just in case, he moves the three of us further into the golden forest. Once he gives it the all clear—and even asks Binx if the ungez senses any other creatures nearby—he shrugs off his cloak, pulls out his sword, and gets ready to teach.

He shows me how to stand, how to shift my weight. His hands correct my hips, my shoulders, and if he lingers just a breath too long each time, I pretend not to notice. But I do. I can't help it. The air between us is charged. I want to back up into him, and when he takes another position to spar slowly with me, moving around me, I'm sure he can tell what I'm thinking from the way my cheeks are heated.

"Relax," he murmurs near my ear as our swords *clink*, our faces almost brushing as he leans in. "You're fighting the blade."

"I'm fighting *you*."

"Not quite, demoness." He steps back, dances behind me, then swats my backside with the flat of his sword. "Your stance is still wrong. You're leaning too forward, giving me an opening."

One he definitely took. Forget my cheeks heating up. Now I'm sizzling all the way to the tips of my ears. "Did you just—"

"Yes."

I turn to jab at him with the sword. Both angry and embarrassed—and, okay, maybe my stance wasn't the greatest—I trip over the ends of my skirts in my hurry to get back at Thane.

He chuckles. "Nice try."

I don't even hesitate. Glaring down at the tattered ends twisting around my ankles, I draw the blade down and hack through my skirt above the knee, fabric falling away to free my legs.

His mouth parts.

"Better," I say sweetly, then lift up the sword again.

Mimicking the way he first approached Morgane when they had their swordfight, I circle Thane. His eyebrows lifting, he matches my step.

And that's when Binx goes low, darting between Thane's stance at the best possible moment. With the bandit's eyes on me, he misses how Binx purposely gets in his way until he's tripping over the ungez and, with a little help from my boot as I kick at him, he falls on his back.

He hits the ground hard, and I'm on him before he can recover, knees bracketing his hips, sword point pressed to his chest as I straddle him.

True amusement—with a notable hint of pride—fills his expression.

"Don't move," I warn.

Ignoring me, Thane reaches up, fingers gentle as he nudges the blade a little higher. "Here. That's my heart. Jab me in that spot and there should be enough time to stun me so you can take my head."

I freeze.

"Only don't really stab it," he adds with a husky whisper. "I think I might finally be getting some use out of it."

Oh, shit.

Heat doesn't just flood my face. It floods *everywhere*. Hurriedly, I scramble off of him, careful not to nick any part of him with the sword clutched in my shaky hand.

"We're done," I mutter.

Thane just laughs, low and pleased, as he leaps to his feet.

"Ah, my demoness. We're just getting started."

THE MAIN ROAD TRAVELS ALONG THE LENGTH OF THE golden forest. Thane said we were heading east, and we did. That's where the Shadowed Woods ended, leading to the travel road. After that, we shift north, in the direction of the Gilded Court—and Queen Celeste's palace.

It's easier to take the road. About five demon lengths wide, it's made up of packed earth worn smooth by boots, hooves, and things that don't leave any tracks at all. The trees pull back just enough to let the bright sun color the path gold during the daylight hours, but once night falls on this part of Noctavara, it's safer to take refuge in the trees.

According to Thane, we're two full days of travel out from the Gilded Court. And though I'm desperate to get to Rafe, I agree when he insists that we take a few hours to practice with the sword, slowing our pace so that the guards give up searching for us.

And, okay, he doesn't add that last part. That's just my wishful thinking that the guards gave up after

Thane slaughtered one of their own. Which is why I shouldn't have been as surprised as I was when we're walking along the edge of the road, tucked inside the trees, and Thane cocks his head. He slows his pace, lifting a hand to catch my attention.

I stop instantly. Binx pauses at my ankle, his shadows pulling tight against his sleek body.

Voices drift toward us.

Fae voices.

Leaning around Thane, ignoring the frantic beat of my heart, I peer through the trees in time to notice a gathering of at least six males in the not-so-far distance. Their armor glints faintly, gold and polished. Crud. It's more of the queen's soldiers.

Thane shifts without a sound, taking my arm and tugging me a few feet further into the trees. He presses a finger to his lips, points at Binx to stay where he is by my left boot, then angles his body just enough to block us from view.

I'm very aware of how close Thane is. Too close to breathe comfortably, or maybe that's because my nervous heart is just about lodged in my throat.

"Stay calm," he murmurs, barely audible. "They won't see us."

"I thought you said the woods were safer," I whisper back.

"They are," he replies. "This is the mistake most travelers make. The queen's guards like their roads. Makes them feel important. So we stay on the edge, watching for them, then hide if we have to. They won't follow us further in here unless we give them a reason to."

One of the soldiers laughs up ahead. The sound is nasty and cruel. My fingers curl instinctively around the hilt of my sword.

Thane's hand covers mine, a silent warning to wait.

That's what we do. We wait until the voices fade, until the road empties again. Only then does he step back.

"You did well," he murmurs. "Didn't panic at all."

"I panicked internally," I admit.

"Better than stabbing me by accident."

I huff, loosening the grip on the sword. "Once! That happened once!"

***

No surprise that we leave the road behind, cutting just enough west that we're firmly hidden in the trees.

Thane glances at me as we walk. "We'll stop soon. Practice a bit more. Find a brook to refill the canteens."

"Practice?" I echo, like that's the only part I heard… and it might've been. "Is this another 'try not to stab me' lesson?"

His grin is wicked. "That depends. Are you feeling stabby?"

Gods, I love it when I see the truly teasing side of this male.

"Always," I tell him. Then, as he holds his arms open, a daring pose if I ever saw one, I laugh. "We stopping now?"

In answer, Thane draws his sword and tosses me a look that's all challenge. "Come, Alana of Sombra. Show me what you've learned so far."

I do.

It's clumsy at first and, oh, who am I kidding? I'm no swordswoman. Having half my skirt missing helps with the footsteps, and it really was an accident the last time I stabbed him, but while I'll never be as good as a century-and-a-half-old fae with two decades of banditry under his belt, I don't embarrass myself too much. Thane circles me, correcting me with quiet words, guiding my wrist, shifting my stance with a hand at my hip that feels a lot more natural than the first time he took leave to touch me.

"Good," he murmurs. "Again."

Sure.

I thrust. He parries.

Again.

And again.

And again.

The world narrows to movement and breath and

the way his eyes track me. Only he's not assessing me now, not really, but rather he's *watching*.

"You're enjoying this," I accuse.

"I enjoy watching you learn," he says smoothly. "And, sometimes, demoness, I just enjoy watching *you*."

I miss a step.

Thane disarms me easily, blade flicking mine aside. It falls from my grasp, and my body moves on its own accord. Part of me lunges to grab the sword so that I'm not unarmed, while the other part… I don't know how it happens, but I end up directly in front of Thane.

He freezes. I grab the fabric of his shirt with my claws, telling myself that I would've fallen otherwise—but isn't the truth that I fell the moment he gave me his unique version of a mate's promise, whether he knew it or not?

Shit.

Close.

Too, too close.

His chest rises with a slow inhale. My heart is hammering so loudly I'm sure he can hear it.

"Thane," I say, not sure why I murmur his name at all, but it feels *right*.

His eyes glaze over. "You make this so very difficult, my demoness."

I swallow. "Hey. You're the one who keeps standing so close."

And I'm the one tangling my claws in his top.

I should take them out before I damage the fabric. My dress is a lost cause at this point, but Thane… I guess bandit finery is made to last. At least, I—

I—

My lips part. A soft breath escapes me. He dips his head and, quieting the frantic thoughts in my head, Thane kisses me.

It's a gentle kiss. His lips are soft yet firm against mine, moving slowly before he slips his tongue into my mouth. I know what this is. Before our human parents bonded with their demon mates, no one in Sombra kissed with their mouths. I guess that's what happens when most demons have long fangs that clash as they press their mouths together. I've grown up watching my parents kiss, though, and I've always wondered what it would be like.

It's *magical*. We're sharing the same breath, and there's something about his taste that has me hungering for him.

All too soon, it's over. We break apart at the same time, both of us staring, more than a little stunned, like we've crossed a line neither of us meant to approach just yet, but there's nothing we can do about it now.

"Wow. That was…" His tongue darts out, swiping across his lips as if savoring *my* taste. "Yeah."

"Have you had many kisses?" I blurt out before I can stop myself.

Not like it matters. He's *my* mate, right? So even if there was a previous lover, he doesn't have one now, and—

"None that can compare." He takes my chin between his fingers, doing the impossible: he stops my thoughts for a second time. "And none that I'll remember after that one."

Oh.

Okay, then.

I suck in a breath, moving into Thane, bumping the bodice of my dress against his hard chest.

Binx—who was watching us spar between grooming his shadowy fur—chooses that exact moment to chitter loudly and nudge my calf with his nose, doing his best to push me closer.

Scurrying over to my bandit, he does the same to Thane's boot.

Once. Twice. Three times. Then, plopping down on his rump, he looks at us both expectantly, his brilliant white eyes glowing brightly as he makes sure I get the message.

I laugh, a little shaky as my hands come up, bracing me against Thane's chest. My palms are flat against his muscled upper half, his warmth doing even more to heat me up from the inside out.

He raises his eyebrows at me.

"It's just… he thinks you might've done it wrong."

Thane huffs a breath that might be a laugh. "Traitor."

Binx bats at the laces on my boot.

"Oh. Sorry. I misunderstood. He says we should do that again. Just to make sure we got it right." Binx chirps, and I dare a look up at Thane. "He's very insistent."

A muscle in his jaw flexes, torn between want and something I can't quite name. Then, as if he's unable to stop himself, he drops his mouth down to mine again.

This kiss is deeper. Slower. A promise neither of us is ready to make, but it's a start.

It's a start, and I'll take it.

CHAPTER 14
LET ME GO

I can't stop thinking about that kiss.

Once we start traveling again, we kind of come to a quiet agreement not to mention it. Basically, that means that I pretend it didn't happen, and once he catches on, Thane is careful not to bring it up.

Hours pass. It's still daylight, and we've already stopped to fill our canteens twice. Before I woke up this morning, Thane instructed Binx to watch over me, then walked along the main road until he found a traveling baker willing to sell him a loaf of bread since relieving the other male of his wares… yeah. Not a good idea when the queen's guards have been patrolling this part of Noctavara, searching for a shadow demoness traveling with a fae bandit. The bread was delicious, though it left me thirsty, and I drank more than I should've.

Which, of course, meant that I needed to pee. Badly.

In Sombra, we have facilities inside of our homes. They work by magic, where you eliminate your waste into a shadowy hole that disappears it before you wash your hands in the water tube. In Noctavara, you find a quiet corner of the woods and pray none of the fae critters are watching as you lift your skirts.

The first time I had to go was so awkward, I held it until it was damn near bursting. So many moons into our journey, all I have to do is signal to Thane that I need a little privacy, and he just reminds me to take Binx with me.

As though my soul-pet would listen to me if I tried to tell him to stay with Thane.

I do pass him my sword for safekeeping. The last thing I want to do is pee all over the metal, and gods forbid I cut my cunt as I squat. I don't even know if that's possible, but if it is, you can be sure that Alana of Sombra will figure out how to do it.

So I move further from where Thane's waiting for me, putting enough distance between us that he won't have to listen to me piss out in the open. As for Binx, I'm used to him being right there, and my ungez certainly knows better than to get in the way.

Once I'm sure that Thane can't see me, I lift up what's left of my skirts, squat low, and do my business. The whole time, I'm telling myself that everything will be fine. It's midday. We haven't seen a single soul since the close encounter with the queen's guards. The woods are eerily quiet—

A hand clamps around my arm.

My scream catches in my throat as I'm yanked backward, slammed hard into a tree. On the plus side, my skirts flutter down to cover my cunt. Then again, the rough bark of the golden tree trunk bites into my upper arms and, yeah, that doesn't tickle… and that's when something even sharper presses into the side of my neck.

Godsdamn it! It's another sword!

"Quiet," a voice hisses.

It's not Thane. I'd be furious if he caught me off-guard like that to engage in more sword practice, though I'd get over it. But it's not Thane, and it isn't just the harsh edge of that voice that tells me so.

The male who grabbed me is definitely fae, but something about him is different. Unlike every other fae I've met so far, he has no hair. His eyes are a deep bronze shade, his too-slender body wearing a pale brown tunic.

"Alastor," he calls, raising his voice and giving me a touch of hope that Thane might hear him. "I've got an outsider."

From somewhere behind me, another fae male appears. This one has dark curls like Thane, and he's wearing a tunic similar to the fae with the sword at my throat. So does the third male that appears, who has to be a slaver. Crud. They're probably *all* slavers.

And how do I know that? Because the third fae male is carrying a length of gold chain with matching shackles at the ends in his hands.

"Well," he whispers, his voice too lyrical for the hungry look in his pale amber eyes. "Look what wandered off the main road just in time for us to find her."

My shadows curl around my boots, flaring instinctively, only to stutter. I haven't sensed any movement from them in so long, hope blooms inside of me at the idea that I could create a portal and escape this, but like always, the magic is dampened.

And I'm trapped.

Again.

I know he told me to stay quiet. The sword at my neck is a good enough incentive to do what I'm told, even if that goes against my nature. But to be trapped… again… I can't stop myself.

"Let me go," I snap, trying to yank free while avoiding the point of the sword.

No use. The hand on my arm tightens, grabbing me and shoving me back in place. Pain sparks down my back, and I spit out a Human curse.

"Got teeth on this one," the second slaver says, laughing, though I doubt he understood what I said. "Pretty, too. The Court will pay for pretty."

Glaring at him because he's the only one I can see from this position, I bare my fangs.

That… was a mistake.

I'm not wearing any glamour. When we're alone, Thane removes it, and since I do feel better without it weighing me down, I'm all for it. We didn't expect that I would go off to pee and run into slavers so, obviously, my horns are visible. So are my fangs.

They may be tiny, but they're there, and as the stink of sour wine hits my nose, I realize that the slaver holding the sword has leaned in to get a better look at me.

His eyes widen, and he lets out a crowing sound. "Oh, ho, fellas. I think we hit the jackpot." He moves the sword a little closer. "I think it's *her*."

No. *No*.

"Who?" I ask, doing my damndest to bluff. "Because I'm no one. Just a halfling trying to make her way through the woods—"

"With this beast?"

My heart nearly stops to see the second slaver holding Binx up by his tail. His fury and pain at being held like that slams into me, and if I wasn't intimately aware that one wrong step would have that second prophecy of Mom's coming true instantly, I would've dove at the slaver to get him to drop my ungez.

Not Binx. Threaten me all you want, but not Binx. Come on, bud. You got this. Get away from them. Get *free*.

For a heartbeat, he hangs limply, appearing harmless. In the next, Binx flips himself up, digging his claws, his fangs, every part he can into the slaver's hand.

On an oath, the fae drops Binx.

Go, Binx, go!

He listens. Though I know he wants to attack the slaver holding the sword, my soul-pet is smart enough to realize that we're outnumbered. Three against two just doesn't work.

But three against three when our third is a fae bandit with a sword of his own?

I know where Binx is going. He's getting Thane. At this point, I don't even care that I'm the damsel in distress who needs to be rescued. He'll come for me. Right?

He *promised*.

The slavers, though, have no idea what's waiting for them. As the one with chains moves closer, chiding the second slaver for letting Binx get away, I realize that they must've taken their own fae portal back into Noctavara just in time to stumble upon me at my most vulnerable. They weren't tracking me, and they don't seem to know Thane is nearby, which makes it obvious to me that they think they got very, very lucky.

And, whoops, I mess up *again*. Focusing too much on where they came from, I forgot *why* they would've captured me in the first place—until the heavy gold shackles clasp on my wrists, the length of chain connecting them together.

In the next moment, the first slaver takes his sword back. Before I can even think of escaping, he kicks my knee, sending me falling to the dirt. The third slaver snags the chains, pulling my arms taut. His buddy replaces the point of his sword, only he has it directed at the front of my throat this time.

Still holding the sword, the first slaver crouches in front of me. "Look at those eyes."

They're dim. I know they are. Glowing gold eyes would always tip the fae off that I don't belong, so while Thane uses glamour to hide my horns, I've done my best to make my eyes look as dead as Mom's. I can't change the color, though, and considering every fae I've seen has eyes that are in varying shades of amber, mine definitely stand out.

He reaches toward my face, intent on touching me.

I twist away, spitting. "Touch me and I'll bite your fingers off."

He laughs. "Play with me, demoness. You won't like how I play back."

Now that he's not complaining about how Binx attacked him, the second slaver stalks over, nudging my hip with his boot. "What do you think? Should we gag her before bringing her to the caravan?"

"We can." That's the third slaver, the one holding the chains. "Though there's something else I'd rather use her mouth for."

My stomach flips so hard, I nearly vomit. I may be

an innocent when it comes to mating, but I'm not *that* innocent. I know the mechanics of the act… and I know how much pleasure a female can give her male when she takes his cock between her lips.

Screw that. If he tries putting his cock anywhere near me, I'll bite that off instead.

First, I try bluffing. Best thing about being in a world of fae who can't tell an untruth? They never know when *I'm* lying. "I don't know what you're talking about. I'm not who you think I am."

One of the slavers leans in, as if he can't resist sharing a secret with me. "Yeah? Well, the queen says you are. That the seers have foretold it. And, know this: the prophecy doesn't lie, demoness, though one of your ilk can."

There goes any of my bravado. Just hearing that word… *prophecy*… no. What? Prophecy? *No.*

"You don't know what you're saying," I whisper. "There is no prophecy about me."

No. There are *two*.

"Oh, I do know." The first slaver straightens, giving the third one a signal to tug my chain so that I'm hauled to my feet while he still holds his sword. "We've brought enough cursed things to the Court to recognize the stink of Fate. Besides, everyone in Noctavara knows about the Prophecy of the Gilded Throne."

As they force me to get up, I stumble, boots catching in roots, breath ragged, arms aching—and none of that matters because if everyone knows about the Prophecy of the Gilded Throne, then *Thane* knows about it, and if he thinks it has something to do with me...

"If she fights," the second slaver says, oblivious to the fact that I'm too busy thinking... *brooding*... to even put up much of a resistance at the moment, "we put her down until we have her secured in the caravan. Right, Finch?"

"Whatever you do, don't damage the horns," the first slaver—Finch—replies. "The queen likes her trophies intact."

Bile rises up in my throat as, suddenly, I'm not only worried about my own sorry rear. Rafe... this is exactly what happened to Rafe, isn't it? Slavers, whether it was this trio or not, must have dragged him from Brille Rouge, bringing him to Noctavara, putting him in chains of his own and carrying him off to the queen.

They don't tell me. Obviously, I don't ask. But I *know*, and, at that moment, I'm so close to offering to go with them willingly if that means I'll end up where I should've been all along: with Rafe.

I almost, but before I can, a sound cuts through the woods. We all turn to look for the source of it: a piercing whistle, followed by a soft *thunk* of something solid meeting flesh.

The third slaver—the one with the chains—makes a confused noise. He sways, the chains going slack a moment before he crumples to the ground, a shining, silver knife embedded in his throat.

It won't kill him. If he gets that out, allowing his immortal body the opportunity to heal, he'll be fine. As long as a tiny piece of sinew keeps his head attached to his body, the slaver will live, but the shock of the injury is enough to keep him out of it for the next minute or two.

The first two slavers whirl right as Thane stalks out of the trees, jaw tight, sword out, and his belt minus his eating knife.

Binx pads at his heels, tail flicking back and forth. He chirps at me, telling me that he's back, that they'll save me, and I realize how ridiculous I would've been to let these slavers take me. I want to rescue Rafe. I don't want to join him in a gilded cage.

The two upright slavers both still as Thane turns his gaze on one, then the other.

"What," Thane says, his voice low and dangerous, "do you think you're doing?"

Finch's eyes widen in recognition. "Aurex. You shouldn't be here. This isn't your business."

Thane's gaze locks on the chains keeping my wrists connected.

His voice is still calm, but no less dangerous than before. Not when the soft lilt of his accent hides the calm of a predator ready to finish a hunt.

"Isn't it? She's with me."

The second slaver's tone turns nervous. "With you? She can't be."

Thane takes one step forward. "I assure you, she is."

His eyes dart over to me briefly, like he's checking for any injuries without letting them see he cares. Once he's assured himself that I'm still alive at the very least, he gives the chain a pointed look, his jaw flexing.

"Lower your sword," he says, voice flat. "Unchain her."

The first slaver does drop his sword, though he leaves the chain right where it is. I'm not surprised. The sword was a ploy to get me to listen. If Queen Celeste really does have an interest in me, she'll want me to keep my head. But the chains... "And if I don't?"

Thane moves forward, his sword flashing.

The third slaver loses his head that fast. Thane drops down, his cloak flaring out behind him, as he plucks his eating knife out of the dead fae's throat before rising up again, sword in one hand, knife in the other, the threat obvious.

Finch's eyes narrow. "The queen will hear about this."

Thane's expression doesn't change one bit.

"That's fine," he agrees. "She hears everything anyway."

The second slaver argues, but the first one

begrudgingly reaches for the nearest lock. He presses his thumb against it, the metal heating up, then popping open with a *snick*-ing sound. Before Thane orders him to do the other, he does, and all I keep thinking as I rub my wrists is: he listened to Thane. Why did he listen?

Once I'm free, Thane marches over to me, grabbing me by the bicep. He yanks me behind him, claiming me all over again, before putting enough distance between us and the slavers that they don't have any thoughts of trying to take me back.

Not like they attempt it at all. Maybe seeing their immortal partner lose his head was enough of a warning, and I decide to go with that. I mean, what could any other explanation be?

"You alright?" he murmurs, too low for the slavers to hear.

My throat tightens as I flash a 'sorry' smile. "I didn't get to fight."

His grip tightens for a second. "Good."

I blink. "Good?"

He glances back at me, amber eyes dark. "If you'd fought back and they'd hurt you, I would've had to kill more of them."

Now that Thane's attention is on me, Finch regains some of his nerve. "You're making a mistake, Aurex. That demoness is worth a fortune even if she isn't the one spoken of in the prophecy."

"You have no idea," scoffs Thane, "what she's

worth. And neither does Queen Celeste, and you can tell her that when you reach the Gilded Court. Without her."

Poor Finch. He doesn't know when to quit. "But, my lie—"

Thane gives him a quelling look that stops the other fae mid-sentence. Once he has, my bandit turns his head slightly, speaking to me without looking away from the two surviving slavers.

"Go," he murmurs.

Huh?

"Thane?"

His grip on my bicep tightens. "Alana. Binx. *Go.*"

And leave him behind? I stare at the hard lines of his profile, the way his mouth is set, and I know I'm not leaving him at all. I'm just getting a head start while he finishes up with the slavers. Most importantly, he doesn't want me to be around when he does.

Got it.

Making sure that Binx is following me, I dart back the way we came before veering left, leaving a trail that Thane will be able to follow.

CHAPTER 15

PROPHECY

Once I think I've gone far enough, I stop jogging before I choke on my breath or get a cramp in my calf. Yeah… I'm not built for running, and though any blisters I develop from endless days of walking heal almost as soon as they appear, I'm gasping before long.

Or maybe that's just because I'm so worried about Thane.

Deep down, I know I don't have to be. He took care of himself long before I arrived in Noctavara. I've seen him, up close and personal, eliminate gold-caps and best other fae bandits with ease. Even though there were two slavers left, he dispatched the third one so quickly, they'll think twice about testing him.

Though I don't think they will. Not when I compare the way they treated me to how quickly they were to listen to Thane, as though his reputation preceded him. They were careful to do what he said. Why? I don't know, and it doesn't really matter.

Not when the 'P' word is rolling through my head again.

Prophecy.

Prophecy.

Even worse, it has a name. The Prophecy of the Gilded Throne. As much as I want to shake it off, tell myself that it has nothing to do with me, what are the odds that it doesn't? The queen sent a soldier to drag me from the inn. And, okay, the slavers were lucky enough to find me with my skirts up, but they instantly decided that I was some fabled shadow demoness belonging to a Noctavaran prophecy.

Gilded Throne, right? It has to be a Noctavaran prophecy, but what about the one that Mom was freaking out to Dad about? I only overheard one line —and, whoa, am I regretting that now—but it mentioned my heart stopping to break a curse. No royal gold chairs included, as far as I know.

But a third prophecy? I… it can't be. It's bad enough that I fulfilled a prophecy when I was an infant, but to be marked by a second and possibly a *third*. How unlucky can one halfling be? All I wanted to do was rescue Rafe, and as the days pass, I can't help but think that he's in even more danger, though I can't see how he's that far ahead of us. If we're taking the same path toward the Gilded Court, and he was only captured such a short time before Katrin told me what happened, he might still be journeying toward the queen on a slaver's caravan.

Unless he arrived in a different part of Noctavara. Unless he's either at the Gilded Court already, or so far away that he's been lost from the beginning. Unless the slavers didn't use chains after they recognized what a shadow demon male could be worth—especially since Thane admitted that the fae in this realm *steal* bonds from demons—and went with a choppy-chop just like Thane.

Thane…

I need Thane. I need him here in a way that I wouldn't have believed a mere seven turns of the moon ago. He makes me feel safe, he knows the strange rules in this realm, and he's the only fae I felt like I've been able to trust—though I'm beginning to think I shouldn't have.

Binx rises up on his back legs, padding at my bare shin. I glance down, looking past the ragged tear of my skirt, momentarily regretting the impulsiveness that had me slicing it off. My soul-pet is sending reassurances down our bond at the same time as he's checking that the slavers didn't hurt me too badly.

The aches and pains from the way they grabbed me, slamming me around, have faded. No, it's the idea that they won't be the last… that there *is* another prophecy that could possibly be about me, and that it won't be as easy as taking off with Rafe and running until I can open a portal to Sombra if all of Noctavara is waiting to see me do *something*… yeah. There's a pulse throbbing at the base of my skull.

In a self-soothing gesture, I reach up to rub my thumb along the edge of my horn only to find it missing again. Thane's glamour is so powerful, he has even me convinced that they're gone. I don't know when he put the spell on me again, but it's back now.

I sigh, then crouch down, stroking Binx's ear instead. "That was a close one, bud," I murmur.

He trills.

"I know. Next time I have to pee, I'm bringing my sword. Promise."

He pushes his head into my hand, demanding a pat.

I smile. "Yeah. Thane's not so bad, is he? I'm glad you agree. I'm thinking about keeping him so he might be around a little longer."

At least, I was determined to keep Thane. During our travels, it really hit me what a gift it is for the gods to bless us with our one true mate. I never thought that Thane was my soul's match until I got to know him, no essence exchange required. I'm attracted to him, and I like him, and though I know it's soon, when I think of my bandit, I'm pretty sure I *love* him, though that could be the bond talking.

It probably is. But that's how fated mates work. The gods lead us to our one true mate, the other half of our soul, and while it might not look like a match at first, eventually you accept that the gods… they rarely get it wrong.

I'm still not sure they haven't. But if he knew…

Binx interrupts my worries with a light-hearted chuffing sound that's enough to steal a small laugh from me.

"Okay," I agree. "If he misbehaves, you have my permission to bite him again."

Binx lowers himself to all fours, turning so he can rub his flank along the side of my boot. I move my fingers to stroke him from head to tail when, without warning, he bounds a few steps forward.

My heart trips as Thane comes striding out of the trees in front of us.

His face is gorgeous, yet entirely expressionless. He doesn't give anything away. Did he kill the slavers? Did he give them a stern warning and let the survivors get away to gather up more slaves? I can't tell, but when I see the guarded look in his amber eyes, I know one thing.

He's bracing himself to approach me. In that moment, I have my answer. What the slavers said… it's true. Maybe the prophecy isn't about me, but there *is* one, and the immortals in Noctavara who know I'm an outsider in their realm believe I'm the subject of it.

Goody.

I could pretend I didn't understand. I could push forward, telling him we have to go, because rescuing Rafe is more important than anything—and it is. So

I've been enjoying myself with Thane. That doesn't erase the worries, the fears, and the nightmares... I'm still determined to do whatever it takes to save my best friend, but if this prophecy could risk my ability to pull that off...

No. I have to know.

I have to *ask*.

"What is the Prophecy of the Gilded Throne?"

For a moment, Thane is a beautiful statue. The sunlight brightens his coloring, a slight breeze ruffling his curls, sending the hem of his cloak swaying by his boots. I wait. I don't know what I'll do if he refuses to answer—or gives me one of his non-answers—but he must figure that it won't be pleasant because he sighs.

"The exact wording is lost to much of Noctavara," he begins. After getting a peek at the look on my face, he runs his fingers through his curls, leaving track marks in their wake as he amends what he was saying. "The only soul who knows the full prophecy is the queen, and it makes sense why she won't share it. But over the centuries... enough of it has leaked that the lower fae whisper of it with reverence while the nobles do anything to quash rumors of it."

"But you knew enough."

He doesn't pretend otherwise. "Yes."

"Enough that, when you found me in the Shadowed Woods, you thought I might be part of it?"

Say no, say no...

"Yes." He thins his lips. "I knew when I saw the butterflies."

It always has to do with the godsdamn butterflies.

I swallow roughly, trying to hold onto my control. Losing your temper won't help, Alana. Answers first, throw your boot at him later. "Tell me."

"Alana—"

I keep my voice calm and steady. "Tell me, Thane. What does the prophecy say?"

"You should know where Noctavara came from," he tells me. "Not the stories the Court tells. The truth."

I open my mouth, and he holds up his hands to stop me. "Please. The history first, then the prophecy. It'll help you understand."

It better.

I fold my arms over my chest. "Go ahead."

"Queen Celeste wasn't born here," he begins. "Millennia ago, she was just another Seelie in Faerie. A high fae, to be sure, but one that was different from the others. In Faerie, the Seelie belong to the Summer Court, full of light and warmth. Then there's the Winter Court, the Unseelie. Shadow magic belongs to the Unseelie, and Celeste… she was a member of the Seelie Court who was born with shadows." He casts me a significant look. "She could wield them, mold them, and eventually she could use them to rip portals through the veil."

Just like I can.

I'm colorless to begin with and I *still* pale. I told Thane… I explained how I got here *and* how I planned on bringing Rafe home. He knows… "She's like me."

"In ways," is his careful answer. "But her differences meant she didn't belong in either court." Just like how, as a halfling, I belong in both of my parents' home worlds, but I've never felt like I belong in either. "Once she found a realm she could tame, one that suited her, she fled Faerie." He pauses. "She welcomed refugees from other realms. From Faerie, from other fae worlds that had split… from the mortal planes, too."

The butterfly, I think. Somehow, the monarch butterfly came here the same way Rafe and I did… and who knows who else.

"But she made a fatal error when she fled Faerie," Thane continues. "She abandoned her mate."

That stops me cold.

"In Faerie," Thane continues, voice steady but stripped of charm, "mates are rare. Sacred. When Celeste rejected hers because he was wary of her dark shadow magic, he appealed to Titania. And Oberon. The true king and queen of Faerie. And they listened." His expression shadows over. "It didn't matter her reasons. They cursed her. They cursed *us*."

Oh, Thane…

"Any fae who pledged loyalty to Celeste," he says. "Any who followed her into Noctavara and swore themselves to the Gilded Court... they would never know a fated bond. Never feel it on their own."

On their own... but what if someone else can have a bond? What if someone else is their fated mate? Suddenly, I understand why the price for demons is so high. If a loveless fae can convince a demon to bond with them, if they can finalize a claim, then they would feel it.

Right?

I don't ask. I don't get the chance. Not when Thane is still trying to explain—

"She built this realm to prove she didn't need love," Thane goes on. "And then made sure no one else here ever could, either. Because few of the fae in Noctavara in this age left Faerie with her. Instead, we were born here, and the only way to survive her wrath and her reign is by pledging loyalty no matter how much we'd rather see her toppled from the Gilded Throne."

The Gilded Throne...

I lick my lips, suddenly nervous now that we're back to that. "And the prophecy?"

"It was a visiting seer who wasn't afraid of the queen, though she should've been. She saw Celeste's future, saw that an outsider made of flesh and shadow, someone forbidden to this world... they would arrive, heralded by crowned wings. And when this outsider... and the seers swore it was another female with shadow magic… when she arrived, the Gilded Throne wouldn't survive."

"That's why," I murmur. "That's why the guards came for me. Half flesh, half shadow… that's me." I lift my fingers, gesturing over my head. There aren't any monarch butterflies hovering nearby, but there have been too many to ignore since my arrival. "Crowned wings. The butterflies. That's why she thinks I'm the outsider in the prophecy. Somehow she found out—"

"Seers," Thane confirms. "She had the one who saw the prophecy executed, but she's kept countless more since."

Great. So she *definitely* knows I'm coming.

"That's why she's using her magic to keep me here. It's close enough to mine to control it," I say, musing out loud.

"She'll do anything to keep her throne. If you're the one who is destined to take it from her, she'll stop you before you can try."

My stomach ties itself into a knot. "I don't want her crown, Thane! I just want to rescue Rafe!"

His expression closes over again at the mention of my friend.

"There's another reason she wants you," he adds. "And why the slavers would bring Rafe to the Gilded Court to fetch the highest price from the nobles."

Deep down, I already know the answer. Still, I demand: "Say it."

"Because demons still bond, and she can't stop that. Neither can the curse. It's a loophole, and proof that Fate will still have its say in Noctavara. Of course, the nobles twist that, too. A little glamour, a little charm… and the demons will bond to any fae that buys them."

Anger flares hot in my chest. For the first time in days, my shadows surge around my feet. "So the slavers steal us."

"Yes."

"All so they can have something that should be given freely. Bonds are… they're—"

"I don't know what it's like to feel a bond," Thane admits. "Wouldn't recognize it if I could, and have spent my whole existence avoiding love when it would only end in tragedy. I don't think the fae *can* love in this realm. That's the point of the curse, Alana. To make you stop looking for something you're never allowed to have."

The underlying sorrow in his tone is like pouring water on a flame. My anger disappears with a *whoosh* and, suddenly, I'm staring at him. And, okay, I'm usually staring at him, but now I'm *seeing* him. I'm not looking at the fae bandit, the impressive swordsman, the charming thief… no. I'm paying attention to Thane Aurex, my mate.

The male who hid in trees so he could look out for danger while I slept. The one who earned the trust of my soul-pet. The one who kissed me, then kissed me once again.

The one who has saved me countless times…

"I see," I say quietly, because I do. "In that case, I know I'm not supposed to thank the fae, but I appreciate you telling me all this. To make it fair, I think there's something you should know, too."

He waits.

"I *do* have a fated mate," I say. And then, in case it isn't obvious, I give him a half-shrug. "It's, um, *you.*"

The silence that follows makes it absolutely clear that it *wasn't* obvious. Not to Thane. Not to a fae bandit who spent a hundred-and-fifty years believing he could never love… but then his lips quirk up, my heart jolts, and the bond between us gets that much stronger.

I only hope it's enough.

So… there's a third prophecy. Yippee. I held out hope that it was Mom's and it gave me some clue how to avoid the whole 'dying' in Noctavara thing, but I make Thane go through what he's heard over the years again to make sure.

And because I can sense through our growing bond that he hasn't decided how he feels about the two of us being fated mates, or the fact that I knew instantly and only told him now, I let him dwell on it instead of pushing him for a response. I did explain why: that I couldn't trust a bandit right away, that I needed to focus on finding Rafe, that when I got to know him, he made it clear that fae don't have bonds and I needed to figure out what that meant for us.

He's not mad. Just… confused, I think, and trying to make sense of his whole world flipping upside down in an instant. I try to make a joke, telling him how I know how that feels—reminding him of my run-in with a snare trap—but decide it's better if I get confirmation on the prophecy. At the very least, it's a distraction for Thane, and, well, I do need to know.

Unfortunately, everything he told me before is *all* he knows. I try my best to quote the line I heard Mom say—something about 'her broken wings' only breaking a curse when 'her own heart stops'... though I clean it up a little so I don't freak him out by mentioning the possibility of me dying in Noctavara—but apart from the wings possibly meaning butter-flies, they're not the same.

So, yup, three-prophecy Alana over here. Excuse me while I puke.

I'm not the only one. Thane's golden skin takes on a greenish tinge for a few seconds there, but right when I begin to convince myself that the idea of being my mate for eternity is making him sick, that crooked smile of his returns right before he swipes his thumb over my cheek in a gentle caress.

"If it's Fate, it's Fate, and I'm not about to go up against it, even if I'm not sure how it'll work for one of the fae and a demoness who are fated." Fated, rather than his people charming one of mine to give up their essence and their bond... "But I told you I'd get you to your friend first, Alana of Sombra, and that's exactly what I'm going to do."

I lean into his touch, allowing myself to enjoy it even as my instincts work to hold my essence back. I so desperately want to give him my essence, to give him everything that I am, that I could ever be, but if I do that right now when he doesn't really understand what a mate bond is… yeah. Not a good idea.

Doesn't mean I'm not tempted, though.

***

According to Thane, we have maybe half a day's walk left before we get to the Gilded Court. So long as we don't get waylaid by any other dangers, we should be in the center of Noctavara, where most of the fae live on the outskirts of the queen's palace, sooner than I expected, given my scare with the slavers.

The way I see it, though, maybe it's better that the journey is almost over. I'm not a seer. I have no idea what's going to happen, only that it seems like Fate has done everything to lead me to the moment when I confront Queen Celeste.

Do I want to? No. Do I like the idea that, based on two different prophecies, we're both in trouble? My heart might stop in trying to break a curse – which has to be the curse on Noctavara—while my arrival in this world is supposed to be the end of Queen Celeste's rule as their queen. We might neither of us survive, but I can't stop now. Not when I'm so close to (hopefully) finding Rafe.

I'm still going. In fact, part of me was determined to walk through the night, determined to avoid slavers and soldiers as the sun sets in Noctavara, while also hoping that Celeste's seers don't 'see' my impulsive reaction.

But that's only part of me. The other half? The essence of Alana that knows this could be my last night with my mate… when he suggests we start searching for a hidden clearing in the woods to settle down for the night, my heart jumps at the chance before my head tells me to hold on.

It doesn't help that my cunt sides with my heart. If this is the last night we have… well, I'd like Thane to *be* my mate, even if he's not ready to finalize the bond. If he's willing to share his cock with me, letting me know what it's like to be his for one moment in my suddenly way-too-short of an immortal life, I want him to.

I want *him*.

My mind made up, I walk beside Thane, Binx hopping excitedly in the space between us. If I had any worry that I was making a mistake, my soul-pet's reaction… telling me that it's about time… smashes them to bits like ash along the shore of the lava pools back home. Just like how he nudged Thane and me together to kiss, he's ready to use his powerful legs and claws to climb a tree in Thane's place so that my mate can lie down with me.

Can he tell what I'm thinking? I'm intimately aware of every breath he takes, every inch he moves, and I've caught him reaching below his belt more than a few times as we head deeper into the golden forest. As night falls, the sun fades to the same silver moon that lurks constantly in the Shadowed Woods— the spot in Noctavara where Celeste first arrived, conquering the natives with her magic, before building her base of power in the bright sunlight. If I squint a little, we're back where Thane and I met, only instead of me wanting to escape the fae bandit, I'm itching to get closer to him.

As though he can sense my need for him through the bond he doesn't quite believe in, he adjusts the bulge pushing against his leather trousers before lengthening his stride so that I don't notice.

Oh, but I notice. Thane… I *notice*.

Eventually, we stop where the trees thin just enough to give us space to stretch out. Over our heads, the stars shine through the canopy of leaves, each one brilliant and white against the growing dark.

I suck in a breath, waiting, *hopeful* as he shifts off his cloak, dropping it to the dirt instead of holding it out to me. At that moment, I know he's mine if I want him—and I *do*.

Binx darts around the tree, presumably to mark it as the ungez's for the eve. Really, he's giving Thane and me some privacy before he disappears up into the branches. I promise him a pouch of snacks as soon as I can, and my soul-pet just chitters and disappears, retreating as though allowing this moment in time to belong to a new bond rather than one that is decades old.

And then Thane turns to me, his eyes heavy-lidded, his lips firm, the hollows of his sculpted cheeks on display… he gazes down at me, and I completely forget about Binx, about Rafe, about *prophecies* as I take the first step toward my fae.

"You shouldn't look at me like that," he says lightly, but there's nothing *light* in his expression.

I cock my head. Sometime after we escaped the slavers, Thane removed the glamour on my horns for the last time. No reason to bother hiding them when other details make it obvious I was a halfling demon —and possibly the one spoken of in the Prophecy of the Gilded Throne that the guards are on the lookout for—but I liked to think it was because of how he enjoys seeing the small, dark points standing out from my colorless skin.

His eyes go right to my horns, a soft groan escaping him as I move just a little closer. "Like what, Thane?" I whisper, my voice husky, and my heart in my eyes.

"Like you've already decided something," he replies.

I swallow, the bond tugging me even closer. "Maybe I have. Maybe I'm just waiting for you to consider what I told you and make a choice of your own."

When he sees how near I am, he doesn't dance

away. That alone feels like an answer. Like he's waiting to see what my next move will be…

I close the last of the distance first. I just… it feels *right*. Like this is my seduction, and the only way that Thane will let this happen is if I take the lead. If I choose *him*. Is it instinct? Is it the bond? Is it because I'm Shannon's daughter and I'll always go after what I want as soon as I realize that I want it? I don't know. I only know that, tonight, Thane Aurex will be mine.

My hand brushes his wrist, tentative at first, then steadier when he doesn't pull away from me. His skin is warm beneath my fingers. His breath quickens, his exhales blowing my yellow hair away from my face.

"Alana," he murmurs, like a warning. Or a plea.

"Tell me to stop," I whisper, then wait.

But he doesn't, and that's all I need to get the nerve to rise up on the tippy-toes of my boots to engage him in a kiss that I've initiated.

It's not rushed. It's not careful, either. It's a holy meeting blessed by the Sombran gods—mouth to mouth, tongue to tongue—like we're both finally confirming something we've been pretending not to feel all along. His hand comes up to my waist, curving it around me, pulling me close as he takes over the kiss.

There's wonder in the movement of his lips against mine. Surprise, too. Plus the faintest tremor of disbelief, like he's discovering something forbidden and beautiful all at once.

When we part, it's only because breathing becomes necessary again.

He rests his forehead against mine, eyes closed. "This," he says softly, "is a bad idea."

I smile, even as my heart races. "You didn't stop me."

His laugh is quiet and rough. "No," he admits. "I didn't. And I won't, my demoness." He hesitates, and then, in a deep, throaty voice that goes straight to my cunt, he adds, "My mate."

I gasp. It's one thing for me to consider Thane mine, but for him to agree? I clutch his jaw, digging my claws into his perfect golden skin, showing him just what I think about that with the force of another kiss.

I break it as quickly as I started it, ready to tell him that I'll only truly be his mate when we get down to the physical act of his body slipping inside of mine, when something catches my attention out of the corner of my eye.

For a heartbeat, I see the glowing white movement and think it has to be Binx. Only Binx is nestled securely in the branches, his face buried under his paws, and the flicker I saw is just about head height.

Thane's head height.

It's a butterfly.

No.

It's a faripoz. The same glowing white butterflies that became my symbol in Sombra—and who have never chased me to another realm before—are here. Because I see one, then another, until a third manifests just beyond Thane, its wings translucent, its outline glowing faintly, the sight of them impossibly familiar.

Only it is impossible. As they flutter around his curls, I instinctively understand why they've suddenly appeared after a lifetime of only following me in Sombra.

Binx had to approve of my mate. So do the butterflies.

My butterflies.

As if agreeing with me, the three butterflies drift lazily through the air until they're hovering between us.

Thane's eyes widen, the white glow reflecting in his amber depths.

"What the…"

"They're mine," I murmur. "I didn't think they could appear here, especially when the queen is messing with my shadow magic, but they came."

One of the butterflies peels off from the others. It turns, flapping toward Thane again.

He extends a finger.

Oh, no. In Sombra, I'm the only one allowed to touch the faripoz; well, Binx, too, but he's also a part of me. Anyone else who tries finds their fingers touching shadow as the creatures wink out of existence.

"Don't—"

He drops his hand, but not before the butterfly settles on his collarbone, wings folding gently as if it's found exactly where it belongs.

It rests there, glowing softly against his skin as I stare in surprise. Seeing my reaction, Thane does the same.

"I don't think," Thane says slowly, wonder winding its way into his voice, "that was meant for me."

He's wrong.

"I don't think," I whisper, "it was ever meant for anyone else."

We both watch the butterfly give Thane its blessing before it unleashes its wings again, fluttering away. Its brethren join it, the three of them lifting higher, lingering though it's clear that they're waiting to see what we do next.

Me, too, butterflies. Me, too.

Thane brushes his thumb over his collarbone, right where the butterfly had been seconds ago. He takes a breath, then moves into me again, bracing my shoulders with his deliciously warm hands. So maybe the fae of Noctavara aren't fire demons, but they run hot enough that a halfling from Sombra won't burn him with her touch.

Thank the gods, even if I can't thank the fae.

"I can't be what you want me to be," Thane says in a low voice, resting his forehead against mine, purposely bumping up against my tiny horns. "But the truth is, I also can't keep denying that I've considered you mine from the moment I found you in the Shadowed Woods, Alana of Sombra."

It has to be the truth. He can't lie.

I smile. "Then do it, Thane Aurex. Make me yours."

He tucks a snarl of tangled hair behind my pointed ear. "But the bond—"

Doesn't he get it yet?

"You don't have to steal me, Thane. My heart is yours. One day, we'll have a bond, but tonight? I just want you." I lift my chin, pressing my lips to his ear. "And that means, tonight, my body is yours."

He shudders out a breath. "I want you."

"So take me."

That's all the permission I have to give.

Gathering me up in his arms with such speed I let out an 'oof', Thane shows off his strength by holding me easily, then laying me down on the moss with care, as though I'm something precious.

The ground beneath us is cool, but his hands are deliciously warm. Steady, too, as they guide me to lie back. Bowing his head over me, Thane looks at me like he's afraid to blink. Like if he does, I might vanish.

"You're so beautiful," he murmurs quietly, as if it's a truth meant only for us.

I've heard compliments before. From Rafe, from

admirers in other realms, from demon males who wanted the prestige of convincing the spawn of prophecy to forsake her one true mate for them. But this… this is different. His reverence makes me shiver, though maybe that's the way his long, slender fingers slide up my arms, slowly yet possessively, tracing the lines while murmuring other compliments under his breath.

As he undresses me, he takes his time.

My coverings could be in better shape. I don't know how females in Noctavara dress, but without my shadow undercoverings, his heated gaze lands on my bare breasts once he eases my arms from my bodice. He shimmies the fabric down to my waist, pausing there before he reveals my cunt.

His lips press to the swell of my breast. His tongue teases my nipple, and I clutch his curls with my claws. Dropping near my knees, he trails kisses down my middle, warming me up to the point that I don't even notice the breeze turning my nipples into points. I almost curse in Human when Thane shifts away from me to remove my boots, but he returns quickly, dipping his tongue into my navel. His knuckles brush my stomach, my hips, and after he slowly removes the skirts of my dress, my thighs. Everywhere he touches, sensation blooms, and I'm already pleading softly for more.

Before he rises, he skims the pad of his thumb along the base of my horn.

I shudder.

He notices. He always notices, and his lips curve in that wicked grin of his.

"These," he says, stroking them gently. "And your hair… gods, Alana. It's like you were made for me."

That's because I was, Thane.

As though he heard my unsaid thought, his fingers sink into the mess of my pale hair. He goes slow and deliberate, loosening knotted strands, cradling the back of my head as he leans over to kiss me again; deeper this time, sure of himself, certain of me. It's undeniable that he's taken over this seduction, that he knows exactly what he's doing.

I refuse to think about how. Right now, I only know how it feels to be handled like this by Thane Aurex.

Distracting me with his kisses, his hand drifts lower, unhurried, coaxing instead of demanding. I breathe his name against his lips when he touches me there. A gentle caress at first before his finger becomes probing, finding the slick entrance to my cunt. I go still, but he's careful, and by the time he slips his finger inside of me, I can only imagine what it will be like when he replaces it with his cock.

That's what he's doing. He's taking his time, ensuring that I'm ready, making sure I'm *wanting*.

"Thane…"

"You're mine," he whispers back, more wonder than claim, though the possessiveness is still there. "I just have to make sure you can take me, demoness, before I prove how much you *belong* to me."

I smile, breathless, but still Alana. "I'm part Sombra demon," I remind him. "Believe me… I can take everything you have to offer."

It's a dare. I know it. Thane knows it. Just like when we spar, I'm telling him to give me more.

Just now, I'm telling him to give me it *all*.

With an arch of an eyebrow, he rises to his feet. His cloak is already off. Without me noticing, he had removed his sword belt with all of his pouches and his blades—including mine, which would've come in handy if I'd had it earlier—and placed it up against the tree. Was he leaving it for Binx to grab a pouch and scurry back up to the trees? I like to think so, but then Thane grabs the hem of his shirt, lifting it up and over his head, and, sorry, Binx, but you can fend for yourself for the moment.

Now, I've seen Thane naked before. His comment that we would see more of each other during our journey was pretty damn apt. There was never anything sexual about it, though that took a lot of effort on my part to resist temptation, but I needed to be clean, and he needed to make sure the kelpies didn't try to get me again.

There's a difference between seeing his body as he wades into water and watching his chest heave, his eyes dark with lust, his fingers trembling slightly as he works his leather pants down after he kicks off his boots.

Once his leathers are past his rear, his cock springs into existence. My mouth is suddenly dry. Talk about a *handle*. There's enough for me to grab, to take, to stroke and still marvel at its golden length.

Suddenly, I understand his desire to play with my cunt, readying me for him. There's a notable difference between a limp cock and one that's primed to mate, but I'm not worried. I trust the gods, and I believe that Thane is my one true mate. Our bodies are made for each other, and even if it doesn't seem like we'll fit, we have to.

I'll make sure of it.

I tilt my chin, digging my shoulder blades into the moss. "I'm ready when you are, bandit."

"Then hold on tight, demoness," he quips, grabbing his cock. He twists his hand, stroking himself, making my mouth water to wonder what it would be like to taste him there, but that can wait. We either have a night or forever, I know that. Still, I want to have him claim me first before I explore the rest of him.

Thane is thinking along the same lines as me.

Lowering himself to his knees, he casts his gaze over me, then follows it with a soft caress of his fingertips over the curls of my cunt. Another swipe of his finger, gathering the moisture there and pronouncing it suitable, he covers my body with mine before lodging the tip of his cock at the entrance of my cunt, making sure we're connected before we begin to mate.

My mate is so warm.

So *hot*.

Thank the fucking *gods*—

Thane begins to move. When he finally joins us, pushing himself inside of me, there's a split second that has me gasping, my claws digging into his back as an ache... a sudden pinch... a *pressure* is all-consuming until it's gone, and I finally know is what it's like to be impaled on Thane's *other* sword.

"Gods, yes," I moan, even as he goes still on top of me.

I must've closed my eyes as he worked himself inside of me. I peek one open, seeing an expression of awe mingled with trepidation as he stares down at me.

"What?"

"Alana," he grates out. "Are you... were you..." He gulps, his elbows shaking, though he's strong enough to keep himself braced over me. "Are you alright?"

I laugh, breathless and daring, my hands releasing his back so that I can slip them into his curls. "I'm just dandy. But is that all you have, bandit?"

For a heartbeat, he simply stares at me, and then he laughs—rich and whole and utterly unguarded—and whatever restraint was holding him back just shatters. He gives me more, deeper, fuller, the bond between us flaring bright and fierce as pleasure crests and falls, all while pulling us together.

Noctavara narrows to *right now*. To the way that Thane thrusts and, now that I know I can—and that it feels amazing to do so—I meet each thrust, our groins nearly sparking as we touch. He's back to murmuring whispered promises, one hand keeping him steady, the other passing over my belly, my breast, my cheek.

I lose myself in the sensation, wishing it could last forever.

But it doesn't, despite my pleas to the gods above, and when we finally come apart—my heart stuttering in my chest the moment I start to climax around him until I'm sure it's stopped beating at all—it's not really apart, is it? He stays with me, forehead to mine, hands steady, grounding, as though he intends to anchor me to this moment for all eternity. As I cry his name into his mouth as my body bucks and pleasure washes over me, then when he buries himself deeply inside of me as he finds his own release… he wants to claim me.

And, without either of us meaning to, that's exactly what he does.

I already told myself that, in his way, Thane gave me his own version of the mate's promise. From the moment I recognized him as mine and subconsciously decided I would keep him, in my thoughts, in my actions, I made my mate's promise back to him.

In the throes, as Thane empties his seed inside of me, I couldn't guard my essence if I had a sword to my throat, warning me against sharing everything that I've ever been and ever will be with this male. I give it to him freely, never expecting that he'd instinctively return it.

He didn't just fill me with his cock and his seed. He gave me *everything* and, in doing so, finalized our mate bond.

Can he tell? Did he feel it? He doesn't say anything, and I decide that that's a 'tomorrow' conversation. For now, I feel the loss of his body as he rolls to the side, tugging my naked form on top of him. He slaps beside him, grabbing for his discarded cloak. Once he snags it, he spreads it out over my naked rear, covering us both up with it.

Only then does he slip his hands beneath the fabric, wrapping his arms around me, holding me close as though he can't bear to let me go.

"You have my heart, Alana of Sombra," he whispers into the night.

I snuggle closer, echoing a line from the mating vow. "You have my everything."

For as long as I can give it to him, that is.

THANE FALLS ASLEEP FIRST. CONSIDERING HE SLEEPS rarely, constantly on alert for threats, I'm pretty proud of myself. Having me close, making me his… for the first time since we met, he relaxes, snoring long before the endorphins and the sensations wear off for this newly mated female to fall asleep.

I don't mind. I check on Binx with our soulbond, assuring us both I still have one with my ungez, and I was right. He ate enough dried meat to have him dozy, though he promises that he'll keep one glowing eye open for threats while I curl up with my mate.

My mate…

Eventually, though, the exhilaration that came from bonding to Thane fades, replaced by a fullness somewhere other than my cunt. It's my brain, and I'm too boneless to understand it at first.

Until, right before I drift off to a well-deserved sleep myself, a vivid memory pops into my head, almost like the visions on the screens in Mom's home world. In the afterglow of being mated to Thane, I try to push it out. I'd heard Mom talk about the essence exchange she had with Dad being like something she called a 'download'. Everything that's Thane is suddenly in my head, but I'm not ready to sift through it yet. I'll have a lifetime to learn about him, and even longer to avoid seeing things that I don't want to—like who taught him how to deflower an unmated female like that—but for now, I'm ready to snuggle up close to him and dream…

But the memory isn't a dream. It's real, and the part of me that is Sombran recognizes it as a result of the essence exchange and our new finalized bond.

I gave him everything I am, he gave me his, and with his seed in my cunt, it's his essence working its way through me now.

And, for a few terrible seconds, my heart seems to stop for a second time—for real as I don't even *breathe*—as I realize that what I'm seeing isn't just one of Thane's memories, but a recent one. I let it replay, and though my heart starts beating again, it's shattered into a thousand pieces before the first thump.

In the memory, I'm looking down at the hairless slaver, Finch. The second slaver is dragging the dead one by his boots while Finch looks up at 'me' with fearful eyes.

"You already took the other shadow demon we captured. You could have let us keep the female. The queen would have paid handsomely for her."

"If you think Celeste will pay when she can just steal the demoness in the prophecy, you are an addled slaver indeed, Finch."

His face goes tight. "Like how you stole the male? We could've fetched a hundred gold coins at the Court."

"Yes, but if I sent him as a gift to the queen, that's more gold off my debt. And you let me because you know that I outrank you. Now flee these woods before I decide to take your head like I took his."

"Yes, my lie—"

"Aht."

Finch bows his head in supplication. "Aurex."

"That's better," I hear myself saying in Thane's voice. "Now be gone. I have a demoness to catch up to."

A demoness… me.

Because he's working with the slavers.

Because he's known exactly what happened to Rafe. He found my best friend with the slavers before my arrival, and gave orders for them to pass him off to the first of the queen's soldiers they found right before he lucked on me in the Shadowed Woods, ready to offer me the same fate if it meant more gold in his pouch.

Because he's my bonded mate, but he also owes a debt to his queen.

Godsdamn it, I think, cutting off both of my bonds so that Thane doesn't figure out just what I've learned of him… and Binx doesn't gouge out his eyes with his claws before I decide what to do. Unable to move, I stare up at the stars and curse silently.

Then I huff out a frustrated breath.

Maybe I shouldn't have been so stubborn about waiting to take his essence and learn all about his motives *before* I pledged myself to him for eternity…

THE SUN IS HIGH, I'M BACK IN MY RUMPLED DRESS, and I have my sword at Thane's throat.

"Rise and shine," I coo, making sure he can feel it. Only when his eyes fly open, his instincts good enough that he goes statue-still again before he can impale himself on *my* sword, do I give him a wry smile and add: "Thandriel."

Thane gapes. Is it the name? Is it the sword? Is it the fierce look in my glowing golden eyes as I glare down at him with nothing like the love I did last night?

All three, I decide as his eyes narrow, though his body stays motionless.

"Alana—"

I dig the sword a little deeper. A dot of gold blood appears at the tip, trickling down the side of his thick neck. Just so he knows I'm fucking serious.

He gulps.

"I wouldn't recommend doing that," I scoff.

He tries again. "If this is about last night—"

I don't want to think about last night. "Hush, Thandriel."

His eyes flash, a mixture of defiance and despair. "So you *do* know that name."

Oh, Thane, I know *everything*.

Last night, my first instinct had been to wake him up, accuse him of finding a way to fool me even without being able to lie, and, okay, cry. I wanted to cry. That's what humans do. They get angry, and they cry sometimes, and when they're made of Shannon Crewes's essence, they get *furious*.

I'm furious.

But despite all evidence to the contrary, I can be practical; or, rather, I can make a plan. That's what I did. Though it hurt more than it should've to stay where I was, curled up on Thane's chest, I didn't move. Didn't sleep, either. Instead, I opened myself and our bond up enough to learn what I needed to about this male before I did confront him.

I had to be careful. I'm only twenty-five. He's existed six times as long as I have. He has the memories to prove it. I didn't want to be overloaded by them, so I only searched for what was necessary.

I discovered that he had every intention of selling me to the slavers if I wasn't the shadow demoness of the Prophecy. If I were? He was bringing me to Queen Celeste himself. I don't know what he did to owe her such a debt, but he was convinced that she'd free him from any obligation if he handed me over to her on a gold platter.

What he said last night to me... that he was drawn to me from the beginning... that was true. Right around the midpoint of our journey through the Shadowed Woods, he'd changed his mind. He decided I was his, but that didn't change the fact that I was determined to find Rafe and rescue him so we had to continue on our journey. And that's what we did, the bandit leading the way.

Of course he was able to, since Thane was the fae who arranged for him to be sent straight to the queen to help with his debt… something he was very eager to make sure I never discovered.

That's not all I learned, either. Like all fae, Thane Aurex is his chosen name, the one he gives so that his true name is guarded. I'm not so sure what a true name can be used for; not yet, at least, though I plan on it. It's enough that the fae refuse to reveal them, yet one bonus of having his essence is that I know what to call him to catch his attention.

And I need to. Because, beyond how much it pains me to know that he so cleverly concealed his role in Rafe's abduction, I learned one other detail in my dive into his essence before I shut the door on *that*, too.

He's lucky I didn't follow his example and just take his head. For the sake of our mate bond, and because his essence makes it clear that he does care for me, I decided to let him attempt to explain himself.

After that, though? To borrow a Human phrase from Mom: all bets are off.

I lift the sword so that I don't accidentally—or, okay, not-so-accidentally—stab him. "Talk."

"I—"

Nope. "I'll start. I know more than just your name, *Thandriel*. I know about Rafe."

His face shadows over. "Alana—"

Still not ready. "You sent him to her. While I've been so afraid of what was happening to him, you knew… you *knew* because you saw him with the slavers, and you recognized the same shadow magic that Queen Celeste used to make the Shadowed Woods. You stole him, and you gave him to her."

Thane doesn't deny it. How can he? I'm doing everything to cut off our bond so that his emotions for me don't sway my heart when my head really, really wants to lop off his, but what's done is done. He has my essence. If he's figured out how to access it, he *knows* how I know.

He stays on his back, though he juts his chin just enough to draw attention to the healing cut on his throat. "I did. Is that what you need to hear? Your Rafe was incredibly valuable. A demon with shadow magic? Celeste would pay dearly, and I never want you to forget who you mated, Alana. I'm a bandit, and—"

My sword is right back at his throat. "Don't you remind me who I mated. I know who I mated." I tap my temple. "I know more than I ever wanted to thank to a demon's essence exchange. You told me that your people force mine to mate with them… you had to have known what that means. Our bond is final because I gave you my heart and soul, and you… you did the same. And now I *know*, and you're trying to justify what you did?"

"Once you confessed that your gods and Fate

herself decreed we were meant to be mates, I expected that this would happen. I don't want to justify anything, Alana, but I'll make it clear: I wouldn't have changed a thing about last night even if it meant I could keep my secrets."

That's right. He didn't stop the essence exchange; it's almost like he *encouraged* it. Not only that, but he let me seduce him. And when I made a move on Thane last night after I finally admitted to my biggest secret —when I told him he was my one true mate—he took over, mating me with everything he had.

"But *why?*"

He doesn't even pretend not to know what I'm referring to. "Because I would've done anything for the chance to keep you, even if it meant that I would lose you once you learned what I had done."

Jerking up, Thane pushes his skin into the point of my sword.

"Do it," he says hoarsely. "If that's what you need, my demoness. I don't blame you one bit. I never wanted to hurt you. So do it so that I can't ever do so again."

My hands are shaking, though not bad enough that the sword isn't steady in my grasp.

"You watched as they enslaved him," I whisper. "You allowed him to be put in chains for your precious gold. And then, even after you helped me, after you told me where to find him *because you knew…* you never warned me that it was to your benefit."

Thane's eyes close. "For gold, yes. For my benefit, always. I didn't know him… I had no idea that he would bring you to me, though I owe him a rescue for that alone. Still, you have to understand… it was for freedom, too. For *my* freedom."

I know. I *saw*. "Because you owe the queen a debt."

They snap open again, flashing angrily, but not at me. Never *me*—

"Because Celeste owns my life!" he explodes. "Gold? I don't want gold. *She* does. Until I can pay her my weight in gold, I can never be free, Alana." Thane leans his head back, smacking it into the ground as another slice appears on his skin. "All I wanted was to be free… and then I met you and—"

I swallow the lump lodged in my throat. "And then you mated me." My voice shakes, but I force myself to get this next part out. "You bound yourself to me while promised to another female," I accuse him. "You gave me your heart knowing you were *betrothed*."

Because that's what I saw. A beautiful fae woman in a white dress threaded with gold. She's everything I'm not. No horns, no claws, no butterflies… she has poise and grace, and it doesn't matter that all of Thane's emotions toward Fiona tend toward frustration, hatred, and refusal, he agreed to the betrothal once… and then he bonded himself to *me*.

His face goes slack, as though he hoped I wouldn't

see that tucked in his memories and he doesn't know how to react now that I have. I wait, and he fists his hand against the moss.

"That betrothal was politics," he rasps out. "What happened between us—"

"Was real," I cut in. "That's the problem. You *lied* to me."

His jaw tightens. He's still at the mercy of my sword, but that doesn't stop him from telling me, "I never said I was honest, Alana. I just confirmed that fae can't lie when you asked. There are ways around the truth if you know them… and those in the Gilded Court know them all."

My mouth falls open at his fae audacity. I mean, he's not wrong. If I believed he was being truthful all the time just because fae can't lie… that was my fault. It's like asking Binx to be a faripoz when he's an ungez.

Thane is fae. A tricky, tricky fae.

I should've remembered that.

Next time, I will.

CHAPTER 18

THE GILDED THRONE

If only because I have the urge to stab him again, I move the sword away from his neck.

Taking that as a sign that I'm accepting his explanation, Thane hurriedly pulls himself into a seated position before turning to me imploringly. "You have to understand. I was betrothed to Fiona during my centennial celebration. The queen insisted. The only way out of it was to buy my freedom from her. With enough gold, there's no betrothal… there's no Celeste making orders that I have to spend all my time in the Shadowed Woods as a bandit to ignore. I never meant to hurt you… I didn't *think*—"

"I don't care what you thought," I snap, digging the tip of my sword into the dirt so that I have both hands to articulate. Finally daring to step out from behind the tree where he was hiding, Binx scampers over to the sword, protecting it in case Thane gets any idea of reaching for it. "I gave you my essence," I shout. "My body. My *heart*. You can't just break that sort of bond with gold. You're my forever mate, Thane, and you betrayed me."

His gaze never leaves mine even as I storm away, pacing in my boots. "I want to be your mate."

"And yet," I say, voice breaking despite myself, fury giving way to further hurt, "you want gold more."

"I don't," he says in a ragged whisper. "Maybe I did, but you… you gave me hope that it's not gold that will stop Queen Celeste. It's golden eyes and yellow hair and the taste of fire on my tongue. It's you, demoness.

"I didn't know why I couldn't let you go," he murmurs, wiping away the blood on his throat as he gets to his feet. "Now I do. You're mine, Alana of Sombra. I can't marry Fiona when I've mated you. No matter what the queen decrees… you belong to me."

I wish I could believe him. He considered me his, all right. So that he could sell me to the queen like he did Rafe…

I give my head a clearing shake.

"How can I be if I can't trust you?"

Thane surges forward, taking my hand in his. "Easy. I give you reasons to trust me."

I squint at him. It doesn't do a damn thing to make him look like anything other than the most gorgeous male I've ever seen—and, no, that's not my cunt talking. Thane is stunning, and I want to believe him, and I don't know if I can… but there's one way he can prove himself.

We had one night. I knew it then that it might be the only one we get to have, but if there's a chance we might have forever…

"Fine. We'll start with today."

"Yes. Anything. Whatever you want—"

I lift my hand, going up on my toes, cradling his cheek. "I want you to lead me to the queen. I'm not following the butterflies to the Gilded Court, Thane. I'm going to follow *you*."

He recoils. Not enough to pull away from my touch, but I see the sudden panic flare in his eyes. "No. Alana, I *can't*—"

Binx decides it's time to chime in. Hopping over to Thane, he bats at his bare leg, giving him a piece of his mind. Thane's lucky. If I hadn't convinced Binx to let me handle this, he might've had an incensed ungez hanging from his cock, fangs sunk into his naked flesh.

Maybe I should've waited to have this conversation after he got dressed. I might've found it easier to stay mad at Thane. Then again, even though the bond's currently blocked, all I feel is the truth in his words and how much the bond's opened him up enough that the fae who didn't think his heart could work is in love with me.

Yeah?

Prove it.

"That's my offer. You want me to trust you? Have my back when I confront your queen."

"I'll always protect you," he says, so quickly that it's another notch in his favor. "But she'll know who you are. One glimpse and she'll be able to tell if you're the demoness in the prophecy that's haunted her for a millennium."

She got off lucky. In Sombra, Duke Haures and the doppelseers had to wait *two* millennia before their prophecy got set into motion…

"That's fine with me."

"Alana…" Thane sucks in a breath. "I know you care for your friend, but I won't let you trade yourself for him."

That's nice. I wasn't planning on it. I mean, yes, I'm getting Rafe back, but I'm saving my rear and Binx's, too. And, *fine*, I guess I can save Thane's.

It *is* a pretty nice one.

I nod at Binx. He gives Thane one last pat with his paw, then scampers over to his pile of discarded clothing. Picking the leathers up with his fangs, he hurries back, dropping them in front of Thane.

"You don't get to decide," I tell him. "There's a reason I'm here. There's a reason your queen is afraid of the demoness in the prophecy."

He grabs his leathers, never once looking away from me. "Alana—"

"Get dressed. Help me rescue Rafe. Then we'll see who protects who."

With that statement, feeling pretty badass myself, I pluck my sword from the earth. A clod of dirt and moss pulls free with it. I have to stop, shaking it off, but overall it was a pretty snazzy move.

Half a day's walk to the Gilded Court?

I'm ready.

Let's just hope Thane is.

I'M FROM SOMBRA, A WORLD OF SHADOW AND FIRE and ash. I never knew what gold metal was until I landed here, but I'm pretty sure it shouldn't feel this cold and foreboding.

As we approach the Gilded Court from behind, that's all I can think of. It's bright, yes, but while I imagined that the palace would be similar to the crystal structure in Mavro, where Duke Haures and Duchess Susanna live, it's not. As though it's made of sheets of gold hammered together, with deep shadows at the foundation, holding it in place, it oozes a warning that a smart halfling would heed.

Too bad they didn't pick a smart halfling to be the demoness in the Prophecy of the Gilded Throne. If Thane... and the guard that tried to take me... and the slavers who almost *did* can be believed, that's me.

Alana of Sombra.

I'm almost there.

I don't ask how Thane knows the way to sneak into the Gilded Court without being caught by guards. His essence tells me that he grew up as one of the noble fae before turning to banditry in the Shadowed Woods. He confirms it himself before I get the chance to question it.

Though he didn't want to bring me here, he's delved deep enough into *my* essence to see that, once I set my mind to something, there's no changing it. Everything he's seen of me since we met only confirms that. All along, I wanted to get Rafe back. The slavers were too afraid of Thane to refuse his order to send him to the queen. Unless something happened to Rafe along the way once he was passed over to the queen's soldiers, he's in there.

And that means I'm going in there, too.

Sneaking in through a servant's entrance, I see that the palace walls are gilded stone shot through with veins of a darker metal that swallows the light instead of reflecting it. Shadows cling there unnaturally, thick and just as restless as mine have been. Just taking a few steps inside Queen Celestes's home, I can feel it: the same smothering force that's been dulling my magic since I arrived in Noctavara.

This is where shadows come to die—no. It's where they come to be *owned.*

Binx senses it, too. Though I offered to let him wait outside, knowing that he would never do so, he stays close to me. Once inside, he presses even further against my calf, his shadowy fur fading until he's sleeker and smaller than I've ever seen. His unease mirrors mine, a low, vibrating warning that keeps passing down our soulbond.

Thane isn't happy about being here, either. Just like when he confronted the slaver, he doesn't look amused at all. Not one bit cocky. The bandit's grin is gone, stripped away by the sight of the Court that made him what he is.

His jaw tightens. "You don't have to do this."

Oh, Thane…

"Is Rafe in here?"

"If he's anywhere, he's here," is Thane's twisty non-answer. He hears it, catches himself, and clears his throat. "That's not what I meant, Alana. *You* don't have to do this. I'll find Rafe for you. Buy him back from the queen. You don't have to face her."

That's what he says.

Fate, however, feels differently.

"Now that they know I exist, she won't stop hunting me. Say I go home. I leave my mate behind… that won't stop them. The slavers could enter Brille Rouge. They can go to Sombra. I'd be putting my parents… my other friends… my *clan* in danger.

"I won't wait for her to send someone else," I continue, pausing only to point at the monarch butterfly that fluttered in through the door we left open. "Even they know it. The crowned wings are supposed to herald my arrival. Well. There you go."

Thane exhales slowly. "You're right. I'm fooling myself, but… love makes one foolish, does it not? I've never experienced it before…" He swallows roughly. "You're right. It doesn't matter where you go. She already knows you're here."

I smile at him, letting my wee fangs peek through as my demon eyes *blaze*. "Good."

That settled, Thane takes the lead. No matter how long it's been since he lived in the Gilded Court himself, he knows how to navigate the narrow halls, the dark shadows, the blinding light flickering in gold sconces. When I ask him where we're going, he doesn't answer, and I understand why. He's bringing me to Queen Celeste because that's what I asked him to do, and he wants nothing more than to prove himself worthy of my trust.

I know we're getting close when a quartet of fae soldiers in polished armor appears in an empty corridor, each one holding a sword just like Thane's.

My mate eases back, covering both Binx and me with his cloak. Under his breath, he mutters, "Last chance, demoness. If they take you, nothing will stop them from bringing you to Celeste. Four against three… not the best odds."

I know. "I'm ready."

Is it a lie? Could be. But I know… I *know*… that the way to Rafe is through Queen Celeste.

And that means I need to meet Queen Celeste.

Watching his profile, I see his throat works, then another crooked grin. "'Tell them that I'm coming?'" he says, throwing my own words back at me.

I shake my head. "Tell her that I'm here."

OKAY. AFTER SEEING THE BACK HALLS OF THE COURT, the throne room is even worse than I expected.

First of all, there is gold *everywhere*. On the floor, the pillars, the vaulted ceiling overhead... but all of it is equally cold and uninviting. The light fractures and bends unnaturally, reflecting off surfaces that seem designed to disorient, to overwhelm.

And the shadows...

Darkness pools in the corners like a living thing. My shadows recoil instinctively, curling around my boots, weak yet angry at how twisted Queen Celeste's shadow magic has become over the centuries, here in her seat of power.

And speaking of her seat...

At the end of the main room, guarded entrances on each side, I see a dais. It's about a foot off the ground, built out of the same gilded, marbled stone as the hallways, but on top of it... if that's not the actual Gilded Throne mentioned in the queen's prophecy, I'll strip naked and live in Loki's old cabin in the shadows from the time when Rafe's dad was a feral demon.

It's a massive chair, completely carved from gold. My rear hurts just thinking about sitting on something so solid… until I notice a gold-colored cushion beneath the voluminous skirts of the queen's dress.

And then, because I have no choice but to finally face the queen, I do.

She is *beautiful*. I mean, of course she is. I've seen the high fae and the low fae here, and as the ruler, she's the highest of them all. I can't tell if it's glamour or not that makes her appear so flawless, but her skin gleams like polished gold, her hair a cascade of pale fire, her amber eyes intelligent and unfeeling. Power coils around her like a second skin, ancient and practiced.

She looks at me—my ruined dress, my tangled hair, my muddy boots… my *horns*—the way one looks at a problem they've already solved.

It doesn't help that she's wearing the friendliest of smiles as she pats her palms on the armrests of the throne.

"So," she says, her lovely, lyrical voice echoing softly through the chamber. "You finally chose to come to me on your own accord."

I stop at the center of the room. Dressed in black like the shadows, their features as golden as the queen's, there are countless members of the Court watching as the four guards march Thane and me toward the dais. Binx trods forward on all fours, his tail swishing, but of us all, I know it's me and the monarch butterfly resting on my right horn that has all the attention.

"I figured it was for the best," I call out, sounding brave enough that, oh, yeah, I have got to be as stupid as Thane once accused me of being. "I don't like chains. And I definitely don't do cages."

A titter breaks out among the nobles. Next to me, Thane frowns. Binx bristles. My shoulders tighten as the queen's smile widens. She doesn't look annoyed that I talked back. Instead, she looks… amused.

Uh-oh. That can't be good.

She lifts her right hand. As I watch in sudden trepidation, her slender, golden hand starts to turn black. At first, I thought she turned to ash, which would make this a whole lot easier for me… and that's when I notice that it only looks like that because she's conjured up such tight, hungry shadows, it becomes more of a gauntlet covering her skin than anything else.

She flexes her fingers and opens her palm, shooting the shadows at the space between us and the dais. As the shadows jump from her hand to the floor, growing, building, thickening… as something forms beneath the shadows, too tangible to be a portal, Thane clutches my bicep and every part of me hums in anticipation.

"Funny," she muses from behind the shadows. "My other demon pet said something similar."

The shadows fall away, leaving a small, cramped golden cage in its place. And inside the cage…

My hand flies to my mouth. If it wasn't for Thane clutching my bicep, I would've darted forward, throwing myself to the floor. Because, sitting on the bottom of the cage, deep shadows under his purple eyes, is…

"Rafe!"

That's all I can see of him. His eyes, I mean. Every part of his skin is covered in shadows, leaving his panicked eyes on display and his mouth unable to answer me.

With the shadows gone, I can see Queen Celeste on her throne. Her smile is still there, but she taunts me with it.

Same with the daring look in her eye.

I try to shake off Thane. He doesn't let me, but I can still point my finger at the queen.

"Let him go! You let him go right now!"

"After all the trouble it took to get him? After all the realms we've searched, and the demonesses we stole?" Her laugh is like a tinkling bell that sends shivers down my spine. "I don't think I shall."

Rising up from the throne, Queen Celeste eases down from the dais, her steps so graceful, it's like she's floating downward. She walks right over to the cage, running her finger down the nearest bar.

"Not that it mattered. I would've sent my people to as many realms as it took, captured as many demonesses as it required to find the one spoken of in the prophecy. Only I thought such a power belonged to me alone. The shadows… it wasn't until my beloved nephew sent me a gift that I realized that it was a wee slip of a Sombra demoness who thought she could take what's mine."

She gestures with her hand right beside me, and I don't know what hits me harder: that she knows exactly what I am… or that Thane is her *nephew*.

One look, that's all it takes. One look at Thane and I know that she's not finding a way to twist the truth.

Oh, Thane. No…

Like, really? He didn't think to mention that little tidbit when he was vowing to be honest and prove I can trust him? No, 'Hey, Alana, I forgot to mention… the queen is my *kin*'! And, godsdamn it, essence exchange? You had no problem showing me the pretty, pretty fae that's his betrothed, but you never thought I should know something this problematic?

With Thane staring at Queen Celeste, I take the opportunity to jerk my arm out of his grip. A second later, I realize that that means I'm free to go over to Rafe—until a guard materializes at my side, using a sword to block my path before I can take more than a few steps.

I stop short, glaring at the guard, glaring at the queen, and then glaring at Thane for good measure.

That seems to knock him out of his stunned stupor. His hand goes to his waist, lifting his sword by the hilt a scant few inches before Queen Celeste tuts, and he yanks his fingers away. That doesn't erase his sudden furious glare as he stares her down from over the cage.

"You say that I'm your nephew, Celeste," he snaps. "The whole Court knows I was your ward. Sold to you by my noble parents, and left with a debt that has taken me decades to even make a dent in." He slaps at his belt, but even I don't think he's reaching for his sword again—and neither does she. She pats her lush lips, faking a yawn, as he grabs his pouch of gold, chucking it at her feet. "There. How much more do I owe you now?"

Rather than answer him, she turns her soulless gaze on me.

"This is the sort of gratitude I deserve?" she asks before turning with a sniff on Thane. "You should be thanking me on bended knee, boy."

If looks could kill, she'd incinerate on the spot based on the force of his stare. "Thank you?" His hollow laugh echoes around the cavernous, gaudy hall. "And only land myself deeper in your debt? *Never.*"

Now it's my turn again as the queen… the same fae female who has my best friend *in a cage*… gives me a simpering look. "Do you believe how he treats me? After all I've done for him."

Honestly? "Yeah."

She purses her lips. "What if I told you that none of it is true? That he's lured you here as an offering, same as my demon pet?" Her gaze lowers, directed right at Binx. "And you've brought one of your own, I see. Maybe I shall take the creature, too."

That will *never* happen.

The only way I can keep Binx from attacking Queen Celeste is by promising through our bond that I've got this. That, even if I didn't, I would never let someone try to take him from me. And, you know what? I feel the same way about Thane.

"Fae can't lie," I tell her coldly, "and my mate certainly doesn't lie to me."

For a moment, she loses the simpering look. The flash of surprise is the only thing that seems truly honest about Queen Celeste, though that fades just as quickly as it appeared.

"Mate, is it? One would think that such a high-ranking noble would tell his queen that he was taking *a* mate." Lifting her hand, she taps her pouted lower lip with a long gold-colored fingernail. "Especially when he has a betrothed to consider."

She gestures, and as though one of the females along the side was waiting for such a signal, she glides gracefully across the floor.

Fiona.

Oh, gods, no. Sorry. Maybe it's the Sombran demon in me, or just the fact that my mom is Shannon, but I am way too possessive of anything that belongs to me. From the books I borrowed from the EL and hid in my room to when I first bonded with Binx and Rafe tried to sneak him to his house, I won't let anyone get between me and mine.

And that includes Thane Aurex.

I tighten my fist, remembering the way that Queen Celeste gathered the shadows around her fingers. If she can do it, and we have the same sort of shadow magic… why can't I?

The shadows at my feet stay where they are, hidden away as though they sense it would be dangerous to call the queen's attention toward them. That's fine. There are more than enough shadows in this throne hall, and before I know it, I've coated my fist in the inky black tendrils.

"Not now, Fiona," I mutter through gritted teeth.

It's not as strong as Queen Celeste's gauntlet. Not as impressive. Still, when I fling my hand out, sending the shadows flying at the flawless beauty moving toward Thane, it works. The dark shadows slam into the bodice of her gown, sending her stumbling back until she's swallowed up by the other nobles again.

Queen Celeste doesn't like that. She doesn't like that one bit.

Losing any pretense of friendliness, she looks at me, fire in her eyes. "You think you can best me, halfling? A full-blooded fae with over a thousand years of mastery over my shadows? How old are you? Three centuries? Four?"

If only.

I jut my chin at her. "I'm twenty-five-years old. A mere quarter of a century."

Murmurs break out through the crowd. Even Thane's head swivels toward me, surprised to hear me admit that. His fault. When I asked him his age, he never asked me mine, and he definitely didn't dig into my essence enough to know how young I was for an immortal.

Hey, halfling here. And, yeah, I know… in so many worlds, twenty-five is still considered a spawn when the race doesn't mature until their first century or two. That's the beauty of being a half-human, though. I'm twenty-five, still immortal, and hungry enough to go up against an ancient fae queen who (hopefully) has gotten a little too complacent on her massive golden chair.

The way her features twist, I think my age offends her more than my audacity at showing up here with my new mate, demanding that she release my best friend from his cage.

Clutching one of the gold bars, giving me a daring stare, she announces to all gathered: "The only way I'll release the demon from his cage, and my nephew from his debts, is over my dead body." Her grin develops a wicked edge. "Or yours, Alana of

Sombra."

Great. So she really knows who I am. Not surprised, considering she already knew I was from Sombra. I don't know if Rafe was the one who squealed before she gagged him with her shadows, or if Thane is right and she has eyes and ears everywhere, but it doesn't matter.

"If those are your terms, your majesty, so be it."

Her lips part. At first, I think it was my mocking retort—and that's when I see a swarm of five… six… no, *seven* monarch butterflies appearing in the room. How? No idea. The doors are closed, armed guards on each side. And yet, there they are, each one flapping their wings right toward me.

Celeste's gaze narrows on a straggler.

"The crowned wings," she murmurs, more to herself than her audience. "The prophecy did not exaggerate."

"Another one?" I cross my arms over my chest, pretending that my heart didn't skip a beat to see their sudden reappearance; and in such numbers, too. "There are way too many prophecies about me. It's getting annoying."

Queen Celeste strokes the bar of Rafe's cage before taking a few steps closer to me. "Are they? Well. Aren't. You. *Special.*"

On the last hissed word, she shoots out her hand, snatching the straggler from the air. Before the butterfly can escape, she squeezes her fist, dropping the broken butterfly to the slick, gold floor.

I gasp. "Why did you do that?"

Ignoring my pained cry, she lets the mangled butterfly fall at her feet. I gasp, wanting nothing more than to go to it, while also knowing that I can't. Not with her sword-happy guards at my back.

But… look. It's still moving. It's okay. Right? A sign of mortal resilience in a fae world, the human butterfly has to be—

Just when I thought it might survive the queen's malicious cruelty, she stamps on the wing with the heel of her shoe. A flicker of irritation crosses her perfect face when she sees that she's pierced it through, the dead butterfly stuck on the heel.

"Griselda? New shoes. Now."

Another of the nobles peels away from the crowd, scurrying toward Queen Celeste. On the way, she removes one of her heels, then the other, so that she has them in her hands as she approaches the queen. Once she reaches her, she drops down, changing the queen's shoes, replacing them with her own before disappearing among the other nobles.

Queen Celeste lifts her foot, marveling at the immaculate heel. "There. That's better."

It's the easy way she killed something so harmless that makes me realize that prophecies… you can blame Fate if you want. You can pretend as though you never had a choice. You did something because someone with a different power than you saw you doing it, and that's all there is to it.

But, no matter if it's a mortal life or an immortal one, we all make choices. And at that moment? I make one even without knowing what the true Prophecy of the Gilded Throne is.

Queen Celeste cannot be allowed to rule any longer. Do I know how I'm going to make sure that she can't? Not yet. Just like how I had no idea what I was going to do to rescue Rafe. Getting to him was more important. Now I'm here, and the only way I'm getting him out of that cage is by going through Queen Celeste.

And she knows it.

As though she can read my thoughts—and I really, really hope she can't—the beautiful yet vicious queen tilts her head, letting her fiery hair fall to the side, showing off the slender column of her throat.

"'From shadow and flesh will come her ruin,'" the queen begins, so obviously quoting something, I know it has to be the prophecy that brought me here. "'She will walk where she is forbidden. Her coming will be marked by the crowned wings.'" She pauses, throwing a murderous look at the swarm swirling protectively over my head and out of her reach before resuming the faux pleasant grin. "'And the Gilded Throne will not survive her.'"

Her gaze locks on me again. "And now you know why you're here."

As if knowing what the prophecy is has changed a thing.

"Yes," I reply evenly. "You took someone I love."

She snorts then, soft and dismissive yet still undeniably feminine. "Love. You demons cling to it like it's some sort of gift. A *virtue*." Her gaze flicks briefly toward my mate. "And yet," she continues, "you stand beside a fae who has never known it."

"He didn't know it before *me*," I correct. "And that's your fault. You broke your realm. You cursed it because you were hurt."

Celeste's grin—no longer friendly, but *cruel* instead—widens. "I *freed* it from the shackles of a bond thrust upon them they may not want. And look," she adds, "I allow them the chance to purchase the bonds they choose. For the right amount of gold, any noble fac female can have your demon friend."

Not as long as I'm alive.

"You will give him to me," I say.

She raises her delicate eyebrows. "Careful, halfling."

No.

"I didn't come here to beg," I say. "And I didn't come to be bought. I'm certainly not paying any gold for the male who's been like my kin all my life." Sensing my resolve, the butterflies launch upward, spiraling in a whirl of orange and black. Binx chitters a warning—for the queen, not me—and my shadows start to thicken around my boots as I proclaim: "I came to take back what you stole from me."

A hint of fear touches the corner of her eyes as she glances at Thane. "Thandriel. Come stand by my side."

Thane shakes his head. "No."

Her eyes flash, glowing almost as bright as mine. "I call you by your true name. Obey me. Thandriel, *come*."

Thane's fingers brush the top of my hand before throwing his cloak behind him, altering his stance so there's no denying his defiant retort. "You don't have power over me any longer, Celeste. Not since I accepted Alana as my mate. Not since she gave me the great pleasure of taking me as hers."

"You would defy me for *her*?" the queen asks coolly.

"Yes."

His answer is simple. Final. Even better, he means it.

She sputters, and I do what I can to draw her attention back to me as I say softly, "Your reign ends today."

Pity she's not about to go quietly…

"Guards!" she shouts. "Grab my nephew. Bring him to me now!"

I almost shout out that he's not her nephew. That he never was. That she *stole* him… but it hits me then. It's not just Rafe I need to rescue.

I need to rescue Thane.

I need to rescue all of Noctavara.

The four guards all lunge for Thane. Obviously. The queen ordered them to bring him to her, and despite my being the demoness spoken of in the prophecy—or that she, at least, believes I am—I'm a twenty-five-year-old halfling who let herself be caught and chained by slavers when she was taking a pee. I'm not the threat, obviously.

But that's only because they underestimated Alana of Sombra. I defeated King Yelios when I was four months old. Who knows what the doppelseers saw me do in Noctavara, but now I'm going to eliminate Queen Celeste.

Whether he meant to give me access to his sword belt or not—and, knowing Thane, I definitely think he *did*—I reach for the hilt jutting slightly from its sheath. When the guards caught us in the halls, they took my sword.

They didn't take *Thane*'s.

He was the queen's… something. They didn't want to offend her, I guess, but that was *their* mistake.

Before anyone can realize who the true threat in the gold throne room is, I channel my mom, remembering how the other human parents would sometimes tease her about the time she stole Glaine's sword from his belt, and snatch Thane's.

In one practiced motion, I unsheathe Thane's sword. Then, remembering all of those practice sessions on our journey to the Gilded Court, I run at Queen Celeste and *swing*.

It's not pretty. I've only had, like, seven lessons, but give a determined halfling a sword, some rage, and an enemy and, wow, you'd be surprised how easy it is to just go chop, chop, chop.

Queen Celeste's head goes one way. Her body topples on the floor in the other.

A hush falls over the entire hall.

I jab the gold blood-covered blade into the malleable metal of the floor. Binx scurries right over to me, standing like a guard ungez at my side.

I grin. "Anyone else want to threaten my mate?"

I'm ready to do a little more decapitating. Later, I'll have to tell Thane how exhilarating it was, but for now, I dare anyone to come at us. The guards must realize that I'm serious, too, because they immediately release Thane.

Because of me.

Oh, yeah.

Alana of Sombra, total badass.

As one, the guards drop in front of Thane. "King Thandriel."

It takes a second, then every other fae gathered in the room does the same. "All hail King Thandriel."

Hang on.

What?

I'm not the only one who doesn't understand. He holds up his hands. "What's going on?"

"You are the only kin the queen has. By blood or not, she claimed you as her ward. As her nephew. Now that the Gilded Throne is empty, it is yours, King Thandriel."

He blinks for a second before a small, slow, irresistible grin tugs on his lips as he walks around the genuflecting guards so that he can stand next to me. I wonder if he'll have regrets that I, you know, killed his ruler/queen/aunt in front of him, but then I remember: this is Thane Aurex. They may call him the king, but he's my mate, and I've seen him chop off so many heads since I've known him.

In fact, when he nudges her fallen body with his boot so he can get closer to me, I know for sure that he's still the male I mated.

Even if Thane swoops his hand around my waist and says with a cheeky tone: "Not bad for a bandit, huh?"

I lean into him, holding tightly to the sword, just in case.

He drops a kiss on my horn. "You know what that means, don't you?"

"That you can order the guards to release Rafe from the cage?" I ask.

The shadows around him began to unravel as soon as Queen Celeste lost her head. It takes a moment before they've vanished enough to reveal the rest of Rafe. The ones surrounding his mouth had seemed much darker—probably because Queen

Celeste or her guards didn't want to hear the way that Rafe had a tendency to chat your ear off—and they're the last to go.

Once his mouth is freed, he lunges to his feet, grasping the cage bars between his claws.

"Alana? Alana! It is you. I can't believe you found me. I…" His eyes go wide, words suddenly failing him.

Ducking out from under my mate's hold, I hurry to the cage, laying my fingers over his knuckles. "I know, Rafe. I'm here. I'm gonna get you home."

"Home?" His expression turns stricken. "Our moms are going to end us!"

I laugh. Maybe it's not the most appropriate time to bust a gut like that. Rafe is still in a cage, even though a gesture from Thane's newly royal finger has one of the guards rushing forward to unlock it, and I just, you know, committed regicide in front of her Court, but… hey. She messed with my butterflies.

No one messes with my butterflies.

While I step aside and wait for them to unlock Rafe so I can finally reunite with my friend and make sure he's alright… and maybe introduce him to my new mate… Thane sidles over to my side again, tugging me up against him. Lowering his head, he places his lips right by my ear.

"What I said before… it means something else, you know."

I tilt my head closer to him, enjoying his warm

breath against my skin now that it's obvious we're both keeping our heads… for the moment, at least. "Oh? And what's that?"

"If I'm king of Noctavara now…"

"Mmm."

"That means you're Queen Alana."

I straighten, and blurt out, "No, I'm fucking not!"

That's a curse word in Human. I don't know how it translates in fae, or if it's my outburst that has the nobles talking amongst themselves, but the room fills with chatter.

I couldn't help it, though.

Queen Alana… thousands and thousands of years ago, Queen Alana was the most fearsome, most fair, most respected demon queen in all the realms. She was Sombra's, though, and our people adored her until she perished in battle. Her mate lost his mind because of the loss, and all those years later, believed that I was his mate reborn.

I wasn't. I'm no Queen Alana… but here, in a realm where I toppled the wicked, heartless queen on the Gilded Throne, maybe I can be.

Still, he saw my expression. Through the bond that I stopped guarding once we walked into the Gilded Court together, he felt my panic, too.

"Don't worry, my demoness. We'll talk about it." Another kiss, this one to my temple. "Later."

Much later.

I know we're going to have to. There's a *lot* we'll have to do.

After all, this is only the beginning of our happily-ever-after.

But, for the moment, I fulfilled one prophecy, hopefully dodged another, and I found Rafe. With the queen dead, I can open a portal to bring Rafe home, and if I choose to stay in Noctavara and be the queen alongside Thane… well, he is my mate. And Binx will make an awesome prince.

Not bad for a halfling, huh?

EPILOGUE

We don't leave Noctavara for another seven moons.

Despite his teases when he was first called King Thandriel, it takes a lot of convincing to get Thane to agree to stay in the Gilded Court. It doesn't matter that, by ending the queen, we also broke the curse that kept the fae in this realm from finding mates. I guess, once Queen Celeste no longer existed, the king and queen of Faerie couldn't find any fae who were loyal to the dead queen to keep up the curse; and if they did, they were careful not to mention it, not with Thane's reputation as a master swordsman. Still, after two decades in the Shadowed Woods... plus too long as the queen's chosen ward, something that I'm being careful to avoid mentioning after catching a few stray glimpses of what that was like for him… he did not want to stay at the Court at all.

And yet, he did. With his new title, he claimed a room for the three of us—me, Binx, and Thane—because I asked him to. Then, because he was still eager to get on my good side, he placed Rafe in a room nearby so that he could recover from his stint in Queen Celeste's cage.

We demons bounce back quickly. By the second night, he was back to being his usual, goofy self. I heard from him firsthand how the slavers managed to capture him, and though I told him how brave he was for protecting Katrin and her kin, I also called him stupid for not making sure the shadow barrier was around *him,* too.

Hey. Brave and stupid… maybe it is a halfling thing, after all.

I also told him that he doesn't need to woo just any demoness. In my opinion, he should be like me and Stevie. Instead of being impatient, he should wait for his one true mate. If it turns out to be Katrin, fine, but after I found Thane… yeah. It's totally worth the wait, even if it's a thousand years just like Dad waited for Mom.

Not like I think he'll have that long to be patient. Maybe we're destined to find our mates sooner. If not, he deserves happiness, and that's something I let him think about while I wait for him to tell me that he's ready to return to Sombra.

I could bring him back whenever he was ready. That's one plus to offing Queen Celeste. She can't use her shadow magic to dampen mine any longer. The first time I tried to summon a portal, my shadows came easily, though I banished them right away.

The reason we ended up staying in Noctavara as long as we did has everything to do with Rafe's hesitation when it comes to facing Kennedy. I get it. While Thane regrettably had to meet with some of the nobles and guards during this transition period, Binx and me stayed with Rafe. I let him know with an impish grin and a whole-hearted apology that I was late returning to retrieve him because I was ducking the mother that was looking for him, and dealing with something I heard mine say.

Rafe didn't blame me for his being captured. After all the time I spent blaming myself, he admitted that he knew better than to stay outside of the protective barrier. He was just begging to be taken, to show off in front of the demonesses, and he, instead, told me how sorry he was that I went through all I did to rescue *him*.

Of course I did. He's my best friend. He's my *brother*. I'd walk through fire for him, and while that wouldn't do much damage to a Sombra demon, I'd take on a maniacal queen, too—and I did.

On the eighth day, Rafe knocks on the door that leads to the room I share with my mate before announcing that he's ready to return to Nuit.

One perk of being the king's mate? When I tell him that I'm going to bring Rafe home, he says he's going with me, and though I warn him that Noctavara was blocked from me once, he's determined to visit Sombra with me… if only to make sure I use my shadow magic to come back to him.

And because he's now King Thandriel, he can insist and no one can stop him. Not even me.

He *is* the king, too. Even if Thane keeps telling me that he'd rather return to being a fae bandit, I know better; from learning him, from his essence being a part of me. As the queen's ward and chosen heir—no matter why she chose him as a wee fae spawn—he saw her cruelty up close and personal. He was forced into agreeing to one day marry Fiona because Queen Celeste thought he hadn't been grateful enough about something else, and he spent his entire existence believing that she would see his head taken before she ever willingly allowed him to take the Gilded Throne.

Joke's on her. *I* took *her* head, and now Thane is reluctantly being the king because he's sure any of the other nobles might be *worse* than the queen. After all, they watched her from the shadows for ages, never once rising up again her, satisfied to make toys and playthings of the lesser fae, the demons, the mortals, and the other folk that Queen Celeste allowed into Noctavara for their—but mostly *her*—amusement.

Rafe was her pet. That's how she treated him, and I'm glad when he's finally ducking his head, rubbing his horn in that way Rafe always did, while his jaw is firmed and his eyes glowing a vibrant purple as he says he's ready to get out of this realm.

Binx hops on my shoulders, asking me in his ungez way if I'm ready to face *my* parents. On the one hand, I made it out of Noctavara alive. On the other, I disappeared from Noctavara as Mom's 'baby', showing up against so many moons later as a bonded female with her fae mate.

I halfheartedly tell Thane to stay behind because Noctavara needs him. He nips at my neck, kissing my throat, making my head dizzy with how much he wants me—and what he wants to do in our bedroom once we return—before making it clear that he's not ready to be separated from *his* mate yet.

And, well, same.

As I summon my shadows, opening a portal between Noctavara and Sombra way more easily than I expect to, I glance at Thane. "I can go to Sombra. I mean it, Thane." Because, to Noctavara, he can be King Thandriel, but he'll always be my Thane. "I still can't guarantee that the shadows will bring us back. You sure you want to risk your throne?"

He slings his arm around my waist, tugging me close. "Alana, my lover"—because he's my mate, but my bandit loves to tease by reminding the realm that I'm his lover—"my *queen*, it doesn't matter where we are. All I wanted was to be able to live the life I chose. I thought that meant freedom… I thought gold could buy me that. Now I just want what Fate has given me: you. Here, your world, any world… just stick by my side, demoness. That's all I ask for."

Behind me, Rafe sucks in a breath, and I only hope that he listens to my advice. He should never settle. True love is worth it, no matter what.

I take Thane's fingers, giving them a squeeze. "You've got it." I tilt my head, giving him a side eye. "Just remember that when you meet my mom."

He stiffens. "Your *mother*?"

He doesn't have one. Well, no. He *had* one, but she sold him to Queen Celeste as a baby fae, so that doesn't count. He has no idea what he's in for, especially when he's face-to-face with Shannon of Earth.

Still holding onto him, I step toward the portal. "Here we go!"

Listening to me as though they never once failed, the shadows spit us out exactly where I wanted them to: right in front of Shannon and Malphas's house.

Rafe stumbles behind us. For a moment, he pauses, like he can't believe he made it back to Sombra after all.

And then, as if his mother has been searching around Nuit for as long as he's been gone, Kennedy appears on her doorstep. Her head turns, hands cradling her belly, as her dead human eyes seem to go big.

"Rafe! Rafe Andrew Barnes! Where on Earth have you been?"

Not on Earth, Kennedy, that's for sure.

At the sound of his mother's voice, Rafe gulps. I turn, squeezing his bicep. "Good luck, bud."

Rafe's eyes dart to the side, glancing at my parents' front door, then to where Thane is glancing around the village square, his hand not-so-subtly going to the sword in its sheath. "Yeah, Alana. You, too."

He shuffles toward Kennedy and Loki's home, but I'm not sad seeing him go. No matter what, he'll be my best friend, my brother, whether I'm in this world or any other. Just like how Mom and Dad will always be there for me, for all eternity.

I just... I'm not so sure how I can explain where I've been.

Sensing my nerves, Thane rubs my side. "You want me to guard the door while you go in?"

And have Thane accidentally behead one of the clan because they approached the house and he was guarding it? In a world where everyone looked out for themselves—except, perhaps, for the camaraderie between the fae bandits—he wouldn't understand the kinship of a demon clan.

Plus, I might need a buffer between me and Mom when she finally finds out I'm back...

"I want you to come in with me."

He nods, and I take a deep breath.

Well… here goes nothing.

Throwing open the door, I brace myself, but neither Mom nor Dad are in the front room. I'm suddenly reminded of the last time I saw them, when they were having that discussion about me and prophecies. I thought the world was ending then, Fate picking on me, and while that's not entirely *wrong*, it turns out that it couldn't have been any better.

I just hope she sees it the same way…

Walking inside, I hear noises coming from the kitchen and I make sure to slam the door closed behind us. There. For better or worse, I'm back.

"Alana, baby? Is that you?"

I pause. She doesn't sound mad. Doesn't sound frantic or worried, either.

I frown, then call out. "Yeah, Mom. It's me."

"It's so nice of you to join your dad and me for supper. I was beginning to think you'd decided to stay and have a meal in Brille Rouge instead. We have—"

Wiping her hands on a woven rag, Mom's words stop short. She has her pale yellow hair pulled up high on her head in a horsetail, her horn-free forehead on display. Like Kennedy, her dim eyes seem to go huge, but it's not because her missing daughter has returned.

Oh, no. Mom is staring at Thane.

Releasing me, he bows with a flourish, capping it off with a wave in Mom's direction.

She blinks. "Alana, sweetheart… who is this?"

Not a demon, I can tell you that, Mom. Not like she can't see for herself. The no horns and sparkling amber eyes and golden skin kind of gives that away…

I swallow. "Um. This is Thane." Then, my mind catching up to me, I think about what she said. "Brille Rouge? What about Brille Rouge?"

"Isn't that where you told me you were going this morning? With Rafe? Heads up, honey. Rafe skipped his lessons with Loki and Kennedy is *not* happy about it." The whole time she's talking, her voice sounds totally distracted as she stares at Thane. "Back to your friend. He *is* your friend, is he?"

"Her lover," supplies Thane helpfully.

"My mate," I add quickly.

More than a few times during our travel, I thought about kneeing Thane in the cock. I know how much pleasure it gives me now, but as Mom's eyes look like they're about to pop out of her colorless face, I have the urge to do something—anything—to get my bandit to shut up when he adds, "Alana is my queen."

Mom's mouth works for a few moments, then she says the one thing I should've expected her to:

"Mal! I need you!"

So you know about the perks of being a fae king's mate. You know what helps when it comes to having a thousand-year-old immortal shadow demon as your father? He takes one look at me, then Thane, and lifts Mom up, whirling her around in his embrace, crowing, "The gods have blessed our Alana, my Shannon. She has found her one true mate."

How does he know? Duke Haures is a bondmaster, but Dad is… well, he's my *dad*. He knows, and once he puts my stunned mother back on her feet, he shakes Thane's hand. Dad's grip dwarfs Thane's in his massive red-skinned hand, but my mate pumps his arm without wincing, then willingly joins Dad in the kitchen for a celebratory javitz while they get to know each other.

I know Dad. While he *is* happy for me, he's been mated to my mother long enough to understand that she would want to speak to me without Thane standing right there. So he leaves, bringing Thane with him, before I can open my mouth to plead for them to stay.

Even Binx hops down from my shoulder, scampering into the kitchen to avoid Mom's reaction and, hopefully, use his cuteness to convince Dad to sneak him a treat.

Dad has an affinity for friendly creatures, like human cats and Sombran ungez. Sometimes I think that he found the ungez himself, brought him to our home, and was pleased when Binx imprinted on me.

I'm sure Binx will miss him—just like I'll miss him—but when I return to Noctavara, there's no doubt in my mind where my soul-pet will be.

Just not when Mom purses her lips like that, the furry traitor.

Once we're alone, I decide to start before she can have the chance. "I have a question."

"I have multiple."

I'm sure she does. "Me, first. It's just… when exactly do you think I left for Brille Rouge with Rafe?"

Her face screws up, almost as though she thinks it's a trick question. "This morning. My turn. What is Thane? Apart from your *mate*."

Right for the jugular, huh, Mom? "Um. He's fae. My turn. Like, *this morning* this morning?"

"Yes. A fae? From where?"

Crud. "Um. Noctavara?"

It comes out like a question, but when Mom pales, she knows damn well that I mean it. "You went to Noctavara? *When?*"

It hits me then. How, whenever we would take a family trip, we might leave one morning, stay a couple of moons on Earth, and come back to it having only been a few minutes in Sombra—or much, much longer. Our trips to neighboring realms never last that long so the time difference isn't that noticeable.

But going to Noctavara…

All along, I thought Mom and Dad were freaking

out that I was missing for so many moons. Looking at Mom's face, it's obvious that—in Sombra—it's still the same *eve*.

I gulp. "Today?"

She blinks. "And you found your mate… *mated* him… in *one* day?"

"It was… longer there."

"How long?"

"Almost twenty moons."

Her lower lip trembles. "Twenty… *twenty* days and nights in Noctavara? And you're okay?" She peers at me, getting a closer look. I see her notice the gold dress I'm wearing, unlike anything the seamstresses in Nuit would create. "You look amazing, sweetheart."

I could tell Mom about nearly being caught by slavers, being woken up by a soldier sneaking into my room, about Thane greeting me with a sword to my throat… and I don't.

"I'm great, Mom. Honest."

Mom mutters under her breath. "I swear to God, next time I see Lucian and Damien, I'm kicking their asses. I'll apologize to Tandy for having to do it, but they're so getting their asses kicked. Let's see if they see *that* coming."

Lucian and Damien, the doppelseers, and their beloved human mate, Tandy, travel all over Sombra in their enchanted cottage. Considering they saw the initial prophecy that's ruled my life since birth, I've often thought they deserved a little ass-kicking myself, too.

But for Mom to say that… "Why?"

She exhales softly. "Well, since you've already gone to Noctavara and survived once… and I'm betting you're going back…" Mom pauses. "I take it you're going back?"

"I… I think so. I mean, that's where Thane's from."

That's where he's the *king*…

For once, Mom doesn't try to argue with me or be her overprotective self. And, while I first thought there must be something wrong with her and was ready to call for Dad, when she says, "I followed your father to Sombra and never regretted it. I wouldn't want that to happen to you, baby," I know *exactly* why she would never stop me from following Thane to Noctavara.

Though she then adds, "It's time you know about the other vision the doppelseers had about you," and I don't know what to say.

So I don't say anything. I just wait for her to continue.

"'Her path is to save Sombra,'" Mom recites, "'but never stay, her fate tied to the one with a shadow for a heart, a gilded touch, and the wrong way… for her broken wings will only end the curse when her own heart stops.'"

Mom shrugs. "I made Damien repeat it again and again until I had it memorized. He told your father and me that it would only happen when you went to Noctavara. And since my baby's going back... I should've told you long ago. Your father had a vision from an old clan seer forever ago that his mate would be full of magic and bloom in the sun." Rolling her sleeve up, she taps the Earth flower drawn in ink on her skin. "He didn't even know what a sun was until he had my essence, but he held onto that vision until the day I accidentally summoned him into my apartment." She drops her hand. "Now you know to be prepared that anything can happen to you in Noctavara."

Just like Mom must have done, I run the lines through my head, wishing she *had* told me about it. Even though I probably would've reacted exactly the same, cursing the fact that there was a second prophecy, if I had known...

Her path is to save Sombra, but never stay... because I did save Sombra as a spawn, but with Thane being my one true mate and the new king of Noctavara, I can't stay here anymore.

Her fate tied to the one with a shadow for a heart, a gilded touch, and the wrong way... That's undeniably Thane.

For her broken wings will only end the curse when her own heart stops...

Oh, boy.

"Um, Mom?"

"Yes?"

"I... I think it already came true," I admit.

Quickly, I explain the first line, then the second—going into a little detail about the Gilded Court, the curse that Queen Celeste imposed on her people, and how it has to refer to Thane without telling her he said 'hi' with his sword to my throat—but when I got to the *third* one…

My face burns. "I don't want you to think I'm exaggerating, but there were a couple of times when I was… with Thane… that it felt like my heart stopped, you know?"

Mom's dull blue eyes go wide as understanding dawns. "You mean, when you…"

I nod.

She bursts out laughing. "Okay. *Okay*, baby. Yeah. I can see how you can interpret the prophecy that way. When… that happened… you must've ended the curse on your golden guy's people."

"Fae, Mom. He's fae."

She waves her hand, brushing me off. "Right. Your fairy tale man. But that has to be what happened. You broke the curse, he was able to bond to you, and now you found your forever mate." Her smile wavers just a little. "And now… now my baby is all grown up and leaving home."

Never stay… "You knew I would have to leave once I went to Noctavara," I murmur to my mother.

Surging forward, Mom takes my hands, holding them in hers. "And I told you to go when you were ready." Squeezing my fingers for a moment, Mom tugs me toward her, squeezing me in a hug before whispering in my ear, "You were ready, Alana, baby."

One day, I'll have to sit with Mom, tell her everything that happened to me once I was in Thane's fae realm. But considering I think I gave her enough of a shock with bringing Thane here and telling her—surprise—I'm mated, I'll wait until next time.

Because I'm coming back. Sombra will always be the home of my heart, even if my new home is wherever my mate is…

Speaking of my mate, either my bond with Thane or Mom's bond with Dad has let the males know that my private discussion with Mom is over with for now. As we pull apart, the three of them—Thane, Dad, and Binx—come walking into the front room, Binx licking his lips as he bounds toward me, rubbing his purring flank against my calf.

"And don't forget," rumbles Dad, clapping Thane on the shoulder as they reach us, "when you two come back to celebrate the gold moon with the rest of the clan, I'll introduce you to Virix. He does the best carving in Sombra. We'll have Alana's name on your chest in no time."

Thane looks at me, raising his eyebrows, before they draw together as something in my essence answers his unsaid question.

Oops. I totally forgot to mention the demon tradition of a bonded male getting his mate's name etched into his chest, the wound filled with a silver ink that keeps it from healing. It's similar enough to Mom's tattoo, but something only Sombra males do.

And Dad's giving Thane the opportunity to do the same thing.

He trails his fingers in the space between his nipples. Even though he's dressed in his finest bandit wear—including his cloak—I can imagine his gorgeous bare chest… and my cunt starts to weep to hear him muse out loud, "You know what? I think I have just the spot."

I'd absolutely love it if he put my name over his heart because, godsdamn it, this charming, cocky bandit owns mine, and he always will, no matter how often he makes it stop.

PRE-ORDER NOW

WHAT HAPPENED TO CHARLOTTE?

I've always been down for a bad boy. But what about a big, bad *wolf*?

I've also always been interested in the idea of myths and magic. Growing up in foster care, never having a real family apart from my childhood best friend, fairytales basically raised me. I was obsessed with them.

Because if fairytales were real? Maybe true love was, too. And happily-ever-afters. To Charlotte Linden, the idea of someone actually *wanting* me besides Goldie was so fantastical that I had no problem believing anything else was possible.

So when a deep-dive into a message board online led me to learning about the forest of Blackmoor? I just knew I had to try my luck. Three days in a legendary forest *and* the promise of a wish?

Sign me up.

Magic is real.

Monsters are real.

Monster *hunters* are real.

And fairytales… they're real, too.

You know how I know?

From the moment I walk into the dark woods, I'm *living* one…

KEEP IN TOUCH

Stay tuned for what's coming up next! Follow me at any of these places—or sign up for my newsletter—for news, promotions, upcoming releases, and more!

SarahSpadeBooks.com
Sarah's Newsletter
Sarah's Signed Book Store

facebook.com/sarahspadebooks
x.com/stressie
instagram.com/sarahspadebooks
amazon.com/author/sarahspade

ALSO BY SARAH SPADE

Holiday Hunk

Halloween Boo

This Christmas

Auld Lang Mine

I'm With Cupid

Getting Lucky

When Sparks Fly

Holiday Hunk: the Complete Series

Claws and Fangs

Leave Janelle

Never His Mate

Always Her Mate

Forever Mates

Hint of Her Blood

Taste of His Skin

Stay With Me

Never Say Never: Gem & Ryker

Bound by the Moon

Sombra Demons

Drawn to the Demon Duke*

Mated to the Monster

Stolen by the Shadows

Santa Claws

Bonded to the Beast

Fated to the Phantom

Claimed by the Creature

Grabbed by the Guard

Taken by the Twins

Shannon in Sombra

Tell Them That I'm Coming

Stolen Mates

The Alpha's Heart*

The Feral's Captive

Chase and the Chains

The Beta's Bride

Wolves of Winter Creek

Prey

Pack

Predator

Protector

The Wolves of Winter Creek: Complete Series

Sanctuary

Watch Me Burn

Make Me Bleed

Beasts of Blackmoor

Trick or Beast

Christmas Eve with Krampus

Just Right

Big Bad Wolf

Murder in Moonburrow

Fake It 'Til You Mate It

Play Dead, Stay Dead

Of Murder and Magic

Claws Clause

(written as Jessica Lynch)

Mates *free*

Hungry Like a Wolf

Of Mistletoe and Mating

No Way

Season of the Witch

Rogue

Sunglasses at Night

Ain't No Angel

True Angel

Ghost of Jealousy

Night Angel

Broken Wings

Of Santa and Slaying

Lost Angel

Born to Run

Uptown Girl

A Pack of Lies

Here Kitty, Kitty

Ordinance 7304: the Bond Laws (Claws Clause Collection #1)

Living on a Prayer (Claws Clause Collection #2)

Diamonds are a Witch's Best Friend (Claws Clause Collection #3)

www.ingramcontent.com/pod-product-compliance
Lightning Source LLC
Chambersburg PA
CBHW020052310726
48970CB00007B/2527